D1554602

Palo Alto City Library

The individual borrower is responsible for all library material borrowed on his or her card.

Charges as determined by the CITY OF PALO ALTO will be assessed for each overdue item.

Damaged or non-returned property will be billed to the individual borrower by the CITY OF PALO ALTO.

P.O. Box 10250, Palo Alto, CA 94303

Other Novels by Floyd Kemske

The Third Lion: A Novel About Talleyrand
Human Resources
The Virtual Boss
Lifetime Employment

Labor Day

A Corporate Nightmare by

Floyd Kemske

CATBIRD PRESS

First edition

CATBIRD PRESS
16 Windsor Road, North Haven, CT 06473
800-360-2391; catbird@pipeline.com
www.catbirdpress.com

Visit our website to read first chapters of our books
and to get further informaiton about them..

Our books are distributed by
Independent Publishers Group

Library of Congress Cataloging-in-Publication Data

Kemske, Floyd, 1947-
    Labor Day : a corporate nightmare / by Floyd Kemske.--1st ed.
      p. cm.
    ISBN 0-945774-48-6 (alk. paper)
    1. Labor unions--Fiction.   I. Title.
    PS3561.E4226 L3 2000
    813'.54--dc21

                                        00-031441

For the boys of JBS
Bobeege, CR, Grif, Jerry, Ken, and Padre Gil
they was drove to it

One

I knew quite a bit about the place before I began my surveillance. Jolly Jim's Refresh & Refuel. Truck stop. Northern New Jersey, just off exit 39. Twenty-four fuel islands, a substantial restaurant, souvenir shop, and showers for truckers – $3.50 for ten minutes under a cascade of warm water followed by a fresh towel.

There's no Jolly Jim. That's just a name. The place is run by Melissa Willard, a well-groomed, slightly overweight 45-year-old woman who makes a career managing Jolly Jim's. I have spent three successive weekends watching her from a rented truck in Jolly Jim's parking lot. I know what time she gets to work. I know when she leaves, when she meets with her shift supervisors, and when she does her receipt tallies. I even have a pretty good idea when she goes to the bathroom.

The Jolly Jim name is owned by a small, closely-held corporation with annual sales of $14 million, 53 employees, and an employment contract with Melissa Willard. The corporation is as closely held as it can possibly be – owned entirely by a well-to-do, civic-minded lady who lives on the Main Line in Philadelphia. Jolly Jim's was a bequest of her late father. The civic-minded lady uses the profits to support various charitable causes. She has not visited the truck stop in over ten years.

It's not difficult to watch a busy truck stop, especially at night. You rent a small truck, drive in, and park. Traffic being what it is, you can leave a truck in the parking lot for up to twelve hours without attracting suspicion. This is my third weekend watching Jolly Jim's. I don't mind working weekends. Some people like to spend their weekends gardening. Some people like to watch or play sports. I like to stalk small- to medium-sized businesses.

Through my palm-sized binoculars, I study the enthusiasm with which the Jolly Jim staff carry themselves under the fuel island floodlights, and I watch their demeanor in the presence of the ubiquitous Melissa Willard. She wears the same khaki trousers and blue windbreaker the employees have to wear and she works alongside them when she is needed, but I've studied enough organizations that I recognize power relationships on sight.

The employees respect her and trust her. It's apparent they even like her. She has been here working all evening, even though it is Sunday. I wonder what the people who are close to her think of these hours. But I suspect she doesn't have much choice. She doesn't own the place, she just manages it.

I have done enough of these to know that Melissa Willard will be a casualty of my work here. But I never let myself worry about unemployed managers.

I am attracted to Jolly Jim's Refresh & Refuel by the ampersand in the name. Is that strange? There has to be some reason to decide on a target. An ampersand is as good as any.

I once saw a documentary on television about a man who studied a band of baboons. He was remarkably patient and would set himself up in a blind near them. They knew he was there, but he sat in his blind quietly for hours and hours, and they got used to him. I feel a little like that man. I sit here in this truck cab, and I make notes on my yellow pad as I watch the attendants running around on the gas islands. I've even givem them names to keep track of them.

There is plenty of truck traffic on the highway, notwithstanding it is Sunday evening. Truckers usually work all weekend. It's a business that requires a lot of hustle, whether you're union or not.

About eight o'clock, heavy trucks all pull in to Jolly Jim's at once. They line up at the pumps to wait, while the attendants dash from vehicle to vehicle, pumping fuel into the enormous side-mounted tanks and climbing the sides of cabovers with their windshield squeegees in hand. They move fast and purposefully and with little wasted movement. They are a competent crew. Lots of teamwork, good focus.

On this shift, there are four men and two women. They are all in their early twenties. At least two of them are college kids. I can tell because they bring books to work. Economics, history, art appreciation, psychology, philosophy. Budding members of the exploiting class.

A kid with sandy hair, whom I call Sandy, practically sprints from truck to truck, keeping the pumps pumping, checking oil, making change. When there are no trucks there to buy fuel, he walks around and picks up litter. When there's no litter to pick up, he reads a paperback book with a lurid cover, which I assume is science fiction. He moves like somebody who owns stock in the place. That's pretty amusing. The person who owns stock in the place – all the stock – doesn't even know this kid, and if she did, she would consider him less valuable than a house cat. But then she's a little nutty when it comes to house cats.

Sandy is my best prospect. When you're looking for the prime recruit – the bell cow – go for the smartest one you can find who isn't a supervisor. They might not have leadership skills, but they are easily disillusioned.

Sandy and the rest of the crew work for forty minutes at top speed to clear out the backlog of trucks. When it is finally over, and the fuel islands are quiet, they all go back to the booths that stand at the center of the islands. Sandy opens a book and starts to read. The dark-haired man in the booth with him appears to be making entries on a keyboard. He is the shift supervisor.

I turn the ignition key to start the truck, flip on the headlights, and then drive over to the island. With the eight o'clock rush over, I will be the only customer, which is what I want.

Sandy closes his book, then trots out to the truck.

I switch off the ignition and watch him approach in the orange light of the sodium arc lamps. Standard-issue khaki pants and blue windbreaker with a Jolly Jim's patch on the left side of his chest and a name badge on the right. Alan.

I climb out of the cab.

"Fill it, please."

The boy is still sweating from exertion, but as he pulls the pump handle from its slot, he smiles at me as if I were the only customer of the day. "Check the oil?"

"It's fine." I look around at the quiet fuel islands. "Are you the shift supervisor?"

"No." Alan turns to look at the man intently tapping the keyboard in the booth.

"You will be," I say. "I was watching you work as I drove in. You work like a shift supervisor."

His eyes light up. He has a fantasy about becoming shift supervisor. Strivist advancement crap. It is the drum beat management generously provides to help their galley slaves push through the pain and row a little harder.

Over his shoulder, I see the plump form of his manager coming toward the island. She stops to speak with another employee, but she is clearly headed in this direction. I walk around to the other side of the truck, as if examining its body. I prefer not to be seen by managers.

The fuel pump is making a soft hum, but I can hear Alan speak to her.

"Hi, Melissa."

"Alan, I just wanted to tell you I think you did a great job with the rush just now. I was watching you from my window. You kept them moving, but you were friendly and courteous. Great job."

I recognize this as a "brief affirmation," suitably personalized. It is from chapter three of *Sensible Supervision*.

"Gee, thanks," says Alan.

"Come see me in my office when you're finished here. I want to talk with you."

"Sure, Melissa."

I pull an IBOL brochure from my pocket and leave it on the ground where Alan will find it when he picks up the litter after I am gone.

Melissa goes away. Probably has more brief affirmations to distribute. I walk back around, where Alan is wetting the squeegee to do the windshield.

"Don't bother with the windshield," I say.

"I don't mind," he says.

"Doesn't need it."

The boy drops the squeegee back into the reservoir and returns to the fuel pump.

"Does she do that often?" I say.

"She does it a lot," he says. "She's always telling us when she thinks we're doing a good job."

"Pretty good boss, I guess."

"Yeah, she's pretty good. She cares about us."

"Caring costs a lot less than a salary increase." I smile to keep the comment friendly.

The boy laughs.

"I used to work for a company," I say, "where they cared about the employees. We were like one big family. We all worked hard and our manager was always there to help out. I really liked that guy. You could trust him, you know?"

The boy nods his head toward the office. "Like Melissa."

"Yeah," I say. "A manager like that is hard to find. When you get one, you'll do anything for him. We put in overtime whenever he asked, same pay as straight time. The people at that company, they would do anything for that manager. I've always remembered that company fondly."

"Why didn't you stay there?"

"One year the company had record profits and all the employees got one-percent raises. After all the hard work and overtime, it was nice to get a raise, but I thought we'd done more than one percent. I did some investigating and found out our manager got twenty percent. I am not kidding. He got twenty percent. And he was already making about four times what any of us made. You want to know why the company gave him twenty percent?"

The pump handle clicks off and Alan nods, then takes the nozzle from the fuel port.

"They gave him twenty percent because he kept us happy with one percent."

Alan fits the pump nozzle into its slot on the pump.

"It happens all the time," I say. "You do a good job and she compliments you. She does a good job, and she gets twenty percent."

He looks thoughtful when he stretches his hand out to me. "Thirty-five fifty-seven."

"That will be cash." I take a roll of bills out of my jeans pocket and peel two twenties from it. "I realized the company judged our managers on their success in cutting costs. It didn't matter if they did it by getting a good deal with a supplier, streamlining a work process, or getting employees to stay happy without raises."

The boy takes the twenties and reaches into his own pocket for change. "Where did you go after that?"

"I didn't leave after that." I walk back over to the cab of the truck. "I joined a union."

A look of curiosity crosses his face. "A union?"

I climb into the truck. "Keep the change."

"Hey, thanks," says Alan. He walks closer to the door of the truck. "A union?"

I lean out the window toward him. "Don't say it too loud. Even a good boss like yours would fire you if she heard you wanted a union."

"I didn't say I wanted one," he says.

"You don't have to want it. Just thinking about it is enough. Management thinks that if you start thinking about unions, the next thing they know you'll be asking for time-and-a-half when you work overtime. They don't want that, do they?"

"I guess not."

I turn the key to start the engine. "She wants to see you in her office. Do you think she's going to offer you a raise?"

"Hey, don't you want a receipt?"

"I come through here all the time," I say. "Maybe I'll see you next weekend. You can let me know if you got a raise or just a bigger compliment."

I wink at him. You always wink at the young ones. They are susceptible to that.

Two

Stillman Colby sat at his desk, reading in the small circle of light made by the lamp. It was just dawn, and he enjoyed the solitary effort of trying to draw something useful from the dense language of an ancient book. Retirement wasn't everything he had hoped it would be, but it did have some abiding pleasures, and purposeless studying was one of them.

Colby habitually read old books. He believed that the past held keys to the present, and he hoped that by communing with long-dead minds he could gain some insight into the human condition. The book he was reading this morning was a volume of Shakespeare.

> *The sun's o'ercast with blood: fair day, adieu!*
> *Which is the side that I must go withal?*
> *I am with both: each army hath a hand;*
> *And in their rage, I having hold of both,*
> *They whirl asunder and dismember me.*

The play was called *King John,* and the lines were those of Blanch, King John's niece. The French were making war on England, and to get them to stop, John had married his beautiful niece to a randy French prince. It didn't stop the war, but it certainly made Blanch's life miserable. What ever made them think that two people having sex could stop a war?

Traffic on the narrow, unpaved roads around Kimi Pond was light to nonexistent, especially so early in the day. So Colby was surprised at a sound he recognized as that of a powerful European sports sedan pulling into the gravel driveway of his cabin. He looked at his watch and saw that it was just a few minutes after six. Headlight beams swept over the translucent curtains on the window.

Buster, lying on the floor by Colby's desk, raised his head and growled.

Colby held up a hand. The dog stopped growling. Then Colby nodded at him.

The dog rose and trotted soundlessly to the door. He stood at the door ready to greet or protect, whichever was required.

The headlights went out, the engine stopped, and there was the sound of a car door opening then closing. The gravel of the driveway crunched twice underfoot, but a warning chime was pealing softly. The gravel crunched again as the footsteps returned to the car, and the car door opened again. Then the chime stopped and the door closed again. Colby knew a man who drove powerful European sports sedans and was always leaving the keys in them. But what would Dennis be doing here?

Colby closed his book and got up from his desk. As he walked across the small room, he heard street shoes on the wooden porch steps. He snapped on the porch lamp, signaled Buster to stay, and pulled the door open. Dennis stood on the porch, squinting at him against the light. He had his hand raised to knock. He lowered it. His expensive raincoat, suit, and silk tie would have been suitable for any boardroom in the country, but they looked wildly out of place on the porch of a log cabin in the woods of upstate

New York. A growth of beard and red-rimmed eyes signaled a lack of sleep.

"Hello, Cole."

Colby saw no reason to act like he wasn't in the habit of greeting old colleagues on his doorstep at dawn. "Hello, Dennis."

Dennis started to say something, but Colby held up his hand and motioned they should go out in the front yard. The cabin, as pleasant as it was for a man in retirement, was too small to contain a conversation in the living room. Colby did not want to wake his wife. Since turning fifty, he had not needed as much sleep as he once did, but she still seemed to need it and tended to be a little grouchy when she didn't get it. In the hierarchy of discomforts in Colby's life, a grouchy wife ranked ahead of a root canal.

He opened the door. Buster went through the doorway first. The dog went directly to Dennis, sniffed his overcoat, and looked up at him. Colby followed the dog out the door.

The dog eyed Dennis warily, and although Dennis smiled, he did not touch it.

Colby clicked his tongue and waved his finger downward. The dog sat. Colby went over and shook Dennis's hand to allay Buster's suspicions.

Then Colby snapped his fingers to release the dog, and the three of them descended the porch steps into the yard. A glow in the east was too feeble to paint any color on the trees or sky, which were uniformly gray. With less illumination, Dennis looked a little more presentable, and Colby had a pang of envy for the tailored clothes and handmade shoes. He missed the posture-wakening joy of a well-cut suit.

"It's good to see you, Cole," said Dennis.

"You too." Colby's voice made a steamy puff in the

frosty air and sounded loud in the stillness. He was aware of the bedroom window not twelve feet away.

"Let's walk down to the pond." He pointed toward the woods. He did not wait for Dennis to answer, but set off toward the path that began at the edge of the yard.

It was the year's first frost, and the crystallized leaves on the ground crashed like glassware underfoot. The pond was not far, and neither man tried to talk over the din they made in their progress through the dead leaves. The dog, who knew how to walk through leaves without stirring them, followed soundlessly a few yards behind Dennis.

As they splashed through the leaves, the gray light began to grow pink around their shadows. It was the kind of thing Colby never would have noticed in the old days. But he'd spent two years in these woods getting close to the world he lived in, and he had studied the quiet gestures of nature, hoping one day to read them as competently as he read the power plays, jealousies, and subterfuges of coworkers. He had been a legend at the firm for his ability to go into an organization and instantly understand the arcane textures of workplace power. But he was a long way from his former career as a labor relations consultant, and out here he was just a man struggling to be in tune with his environment.

There were few opportunities to use his gift in these woods, but living here had not dulled it. Years of training stirred in him, and he sensed that he held the power in the conversation they were going to have. He would be generous with it. It was a technique that had never failed him.

By the time they reached the pond, the sun was just above the horizon behind them. It painted a great orange spot on the glassy water. Vapor rose from the water beyond this reflection, making the gleaming opaque surface look solid, like a dance floor in paradise. The angels were all sitting this one out, however, and nothing disturbed the smooth surface. A flock of honking geese overhead, like airborne bicycle horns, wheeled southward and slowly faded from earshot.

People who speak English, unless they feel very much at ease with each other, will not allow a conversational silence to last longer than four seconds. But Colby had long ago trained himself to tolerate conversational discomfort. More than once he'd gained critical information in that fourth second. Now he counted the seconds of silence as he watched Dennis's face in the feeble red light of the rising sun. One thousand one, one thousand two, one thousand three, one thousand four.

"How's Frannie?" said Dennis.

"She's fine," said Colby.

"Pretty as ever?"

Colby wondered if there was some subtext to Dennis's inquiry. But he looked at him, and Dennis's expression was open and pleasant. He intended it as a compliment, whether for Frannie or Colby himself it was difficult to tell.

Dennis didn't wait for an answer, but continued with his small talk. "Nice dog," he said. "What kind is it?"

"He doesn't have a kind," said Colby. "He came from a shelter. His name's Buster."

At the sound of his name, the dog glanced back at Colby, then returned to his surveillance of Dennis.

Dennis looked around at the woods and the pond. "Beautiful out here."

It was Colby's turn, but he did not reply. One thousand one, one thousand two, one thousand three, one thousand four.

"What have you been doing?" said Dennis.

Colby was surprised that Dennis had chosen to go right into phase one. Get the other guy to talk about himself.

"Dog training," said Colby. He clicked his tongue. The dog trotted over and sat beside him.

"It takes a lot of patience, I understand," said Dennis.

"Depends on the dog," said Colby.

"Like a consulting assignment, right?" said Dennis.

Colby nodded. "Every dog is an individual, but you always approach them in the same way."

"Which way is that?"

"You and the dog become a dog pack," said Colby.

Dennis laughed. "A dog pack with two members. That's funny." He picked up a stone. The dog growled.

Colby clicked his tongue and raised his hand.

Dennis looked at the dog.

"It's OK," said Colby. "He won't bother you."

Dennis threw the stone skyward.

Colby and the dog watched the stone arc through the sky then plunge downward toward the pond to strike the center of the reflected sun.

"What do you do for excitement out here?" said Dennis.

"I mostly try to avoid excitement." Colby knew that the less he said in this conversation, the more control he had of it.

One thousand one. One thousand two. His patience was rewarded.

"Is that why you live in the woods?" said Dennis.

He had forced Dennis's opener. Colby felt a tiny thrill. For an instant, he could almost feel the jacket of his Brooks Brothers suit across his shoulders and the weight of his Waterman pen in the inside pocket.

"I live in the woods because it's good for my marriage."

Dennis nodded his understanding. "I guess you don't have many arguments out here."

"Frannie stays out of the affairs of her local, and I never talk about the old life."

Dennis looked down at the ground. The silence became uncomfortable before he spoke again. "Sometimes I envy you, Cole. Being out here, surrounded by nature, living in the peace and quiet."

"You don't have to envy me, Dennis." Colby released Buster, who walked away to sniff at unseen things among the dead leaves. "You could live out here if you wanted. It's just a matter of making your mind up about what's important." Colby watched Buster follow an unknown scent. "We live simply but happily here. Frannie has her kindergartners, and I have my studies. We can even afford a restaurant meal over in Mount Paley from time to time."

"Dennis looked up and stared at him a moment without saying anything, as if assessing the best approach to getting what he wanted. Finally he spoke.

"Do you get the *Journal* out here, Cole?"

Colby shook his head. "The *Wall Street Journal* is a little too expensive for me. We don't have cable, and I don't have a net account. The nearest radio station carries nothing but farm reports and conversation for shut-ins."

"Then I guess you don't know what happened at Growth Services," said Dennis.

Interest stirred in Colby like lust. The first time he had beaten the FOW – Federated Office Workers – in an RC election was at Growth Services. It had been a milestone of his career, and in many ways it had defined his destiny. That personal triumph had locked him into a lifelong professional feud with Harvey Lathrop, president of the FOW. The feud had only ended when Lathrop beat him soundly a decade later in an RC election at Consequential, Inc. It had been Colby's last assignment.

"Something happened to Growth Services?"

"They've been union for two weeks now."

Union? Colby felt like he'd been informed of the death of a friend. He wondered if Harvey Lathrop had done it. "FOW?"

Dennis smiled, and Colby realized he had fallen into his old habit of pronouncing the name of the union as *foul*. Colby waited for the other man to answer.

"They call themselves the IBOL." Dennis pronounced the letters individually. "International Brotherhood of Labor. Last quarter, Growth Services was named in a petition. By the time they called us, the union had gotten signed cards from eighty percent of their employees. We tried to stop it, but the election was tough."

"Never heard of the IBOL."

"Nobody had," said Dennis. "They just came out of nowhere."

The two men and the dog stood silently for a moment before Colby spoke again.

"What do you have on them?"

"Zip," said Dennis. "We haven't even been able to find their headquarters. They haven't filed with the IRS, they have no mailing permits, and the Labor Department never heard of them."

Colby wondered how they did any organizing without a mailing permit.

"We think they may have outsourced the organizing effort," said Dennis.

"You mean freelancers?"

Dennis held a single finger in the air. "A freelancer. The guy's a pro, Cole. Nobody has admitted to seeing him. The workers claimed it was completely spontaneous. Like they were just doing their jobs one day, and the next day decided they wanted a union and that union was the IBOL."

"Any chance they're telling the truth?"

"Oh, come on," said Dennis. "This was a small workforce of intelligent, well-educated people. Morale was good, productivity was rising. Management thought everything was fine. Bang! They get a call from somebody saying he represents the IBOL, and it's off to the races."

It didn't sound like any organizing effort Colby had ever seen. Had the world turned upside-down in the years since he'd retired?

"Growth Services was the first," said Dennis. "But there are others. The IBOL has been turning up in a lot of places, some of them pretty strange."

"What do you want from me, Dennis?" said Colby.

Dennis turned and threw another stone into the pond. "We have a new client."

It was not like Dennis to be so roundabout. Colby sensed that he was exercising special care in this negotiation.

"Do you remember Harvey Lathrop?" Dennis tossed another stone into the pond.

How could Dennis suspect Colby might have forgotten Lathrop, the man who'd been responsible for his early retirement? Colby had never met Lathrop in person, but he knew him intimately, as only a lifelong enemy can.

Dennis turned his gaze away from the outward spreading ripples in the pond and looked at Colby seriously. "Harvey Lathrop is the IBOL's next target."

"What do you mean?"

"The IBOL freelancer is trying to organize the headquarters staff of the FOW," said Dennis. "Harvey Lathrop is our newest client."

Colby would have preferred to maintain his decorum, but laughter exploded from his chest and throat like a coughing fit. Harvey Lathrop the target of a union organizing drive! It seemed to prove there was a God. He continued to laugh for a moment, but he saw that Dennis was staring at him seriously. He got control of himself.

"Don't you see the humor in this, Dennis?"

Dennis still wore a serious look. "He's a client, Cole."

"And how did that happen?" said Colby. "My God, the man has spent his life fighting us. He's been responsible for most of the firm's failures." Even as he spoke, Colby realized he was talking about himself more than the firm.

"A client is a client," said Dennis simply. "He needs us for what we do best."

And then Colby felt small for allowing his feelings to color his view of what was after all a business matter. Dennis was right. It was the firm's business to minister to those in need, regardless of industry, politics, or past activities. To ignore Harvey Lathrop's need would be a betrayal of the values they both prized.

But Harvey Lathrop was Dennis's problem. Colby was retired and entitled to enjoy the situation. He smiled again. "I'd like to see that election."

"I'd like you to see it, too," said Dennis. "That's why I'm here."

Suddenly Colby understood what was going on. Dennis was here to get him to take an assignment, the assignment to fight a union at the headquarters of the FOW. "You're kidding."

"No, I'm not," said Dennis. "I've never been more serious."

"Why me?" said Colby. "Surely you have some energetic and serious young people who would love the challenge and could do the work with a straight face."

"Maybe," said Dennis. "But Harvey Lathrop asked for you. He said he wanted the best."

* * *

After Frannie left for work that morning, Colby did not go back to *King John*. He simply sat down in the living room for a moment to savor his meeting with Dennis. He had turned down the assignment, of course. But to hear his work and his abilities praised by a lifelong adversary! Colby felt he could permit himself to enjoy it a little before going back to his studies. *King John* was not, after all, Shakespeare's best work, and in moments of honesty Colby admitted to himself that it was tedious to read.

On an impulse, he began rummaging in his desk drawer until he found a small key of stamped metal. He went to the closet of the bedroom and made his way through a small forest of coats and jackets to the trunk that sat on the floor. He dragged it out of the closet, took the key, and unlocked it. He felt his heart begin to race when he lifted the lid. His calfskin briefcase lay on top. He took it out and set it aside. Beneath it was a plastic garment bag. He took this out and laid it on the bed.

When he opened the bag, the odor of mothballs was strong. He pulled the dark blue suit on its wooden coat hanger from the bag and draped it on the bedspread to air out. One of the pocket flaps was creased, so that its corner stuck out at an angle. There was a flowered yellow necktie and a pair of silk suspenders draped over the shoulders. A silk handkerchief protruded from the breast pocket. The handkerchief was crimson, and it matched one of the minor colors of the necktie pattern. He pulled the lap aside and there was the familiar suspended sheep of the Brooks Brothers emblem sewn to the inside pocket.

He heard the dog barking in the front yard and went to the living room window to see what was going on. The dog stood in the center of the yard, barking at nothing. Colby had seen him do this before. He seemed to enjoy it. But Colby had been working with him on the barking because he wanted Buster to learn to bark at danger rather than for recreation. Colby opened the window.

"Buster, hush," he said.

The dog stopped barking to turn and look at him.

"Good dog." Colby closed the window.

The dog turned back to look at the woods. But he didn't bark again.

Colby went back into the bedroom. The suit lay on the bed like a deflated consultant. Colby kicked off his shoes and took off his sweatshirt and jeans. Then he took the suit's pants from the hanger, and began fastening the suspenders to the buttons on the inside of the waistband. When he had all six buttons fastened, he stepped into the trousers. He had not put on a shirt, and he felt rather silly pulling the suspenders on to his shoulders over his tee shirt. And when he looked at himself in the mirror over the bedroom bureau, he saw that he looked just as silly as he felt.

He allowed himself another moment of pride that the trousers fit so well. He had kept himself in good shape. He put a thumb under his right suspender to take it off, but he saw the jacket still lying on the bed, so he left the suspender over his shoulder, walked over to the bed, and donned the jacket. The feeling of silliness evaporated. The dark blue jacket settled on to his shoulders like a harness. It pulled his shoulders back, thrust his chest out, and charged his entire body with an inexpressible energy.

He'd been wearing a suit like this the day they had won against the FOW at Growth Services. He remembered Cynthia Price's speech to the management staff, in which she'd congratulated them on their good work. Everybody was giddy with the victory, and in response to the CEO's prodding they had applauded themselves, albeit playfully. And then the CEO had introduced Colby.

"Ladies and gentlemen," she said, "I give you the hero of Growth Services, Inc., Stillman Colby."

The crowd had roared. There were whistles and cheers, and Colby had walked out onto the dais and stood there, slightly embarrassed, while they clapped and shouted with the giddiness of sudden relaxation. The cheering had gone on and on. It rang in Colby's ears, until it was drowned out by the sound of his dog barking in the front yard.

* * *

It had turned warm again. There were no blankets on the bed, just a sheet. Both Colby and Frannie uncovered their naked torsos. The bedroom curtains were open, and the full moon flooded the room with light. Colby couldn't sleep. He pushed himself up on his elbow and looked over at Frannie on the other side of the bed. Her eyes were closed, but her breathing was deep, and he knew she was awake.

As if she felt him staring at her, she spoke.

"I hope you're not thinking about going back to it, Still."

People he worked with always called him "Cole." Only Frannie shortened his first name, Stillman.

"Going back to what?" said Colby, although he knew very well what she meant.

"You want to do it, don't you?" Frannie rolled over on her side, opened her eyes, and faced him.

"No," said Colby. "I want to stay here with you. But they need me, Frannie. Your old union needs me."

It was the first time in years that Colby had spoken about Frannie's union activities.

"I know what you're doing, Still."

Colby realized he had said the wrong thing, and now he'd never be able to take it back. They'd had a great life these past few years, but only because there was one topic they never talked about.

"We both know why you want to do it," said Frannie, "and it doesn't have anything to do with saving my old union. You want to put on one of your Brooks Brothers suits and drive around in a fancy car."

Colby knew she was upset. She hadn't used that belittling tone with him since they'd left the city. It annoyed him. "Harvey Lathrop asked for me."

"So there it is," she said. "It's the glands. The guy who beat you has asked for your help, and you want to rub his face in it."

Frannie had a certain amount of bitterness about Colby's former profession, which she associated, like everything else she found problematical about him, with his maleness.

"Lathrop is an important strategic objective for them," he said at last.

"Can't you talk like a normal human being?" She rolled away from him to face the wall.

Colby didn't think there was anything abnormal in his remark, but experience told him she was referring to the phrase "important strategic objective." He felt like arguing the point, but he knew if he did, it would confirm her belief he was in the grip of his hormones.

"I don't want to leave," he said. "I want to stay here with you."

"Forget it, Still," she said to the wall. "I know where this is leading."

He touched her shoulder. "Where?"

She continued to speak to the wall. "You're going to tell me that if somebody doesn't stop this union, the world will come to an end." She rolled back over to face him.

"I didn't say the world was going to end," said Colby lamely. Frannie had a way of misrepresenting his thoughts and making *him* feel small for having the thoughts that inspired her misinterpretations. It occurred to him that if he didn't love Frannie, he might not like her. She had a mean streak that he sometimes found upsetting.

"They've aleady taken Growth Services," he said, "and it looks like they are seeking control of the FOW. It's a critical milestone in their plan." He was careful to say the name of the union as initials.

Frannie looked at him as if he were one of her more inept kindergartners. "What does that mean, a critical milestone in their plan?"

Colby's ears burned. It sounded silly when Frannie said it.

They stared at each other in the moonlight. Then Colby saw a streak of silver on her cheek, and he knew she was crying, whether from sadness or anger he couldn't tell. He reached out to touch the streak left by the tear, but she grabbed his hand. She gripped it hard, and he thought she was going to push it away, but she pressed it to her bare breast. Without thinking about it, without even willing it, he laid himself down on top of her and embraced her.

"You son of a bitch," she hissed as she pulled the sheet from between them and spread her legs.

Colby thought it best not to speak. He entered her, then concentrated on thrusting himself into her. There was no foreplay, no caressing – just two bodies groping and pounding and squeezing. There was nothing submissive about her. She was soft on the outside, but below the surface she was strong and willful as the most hard-bitten labor boss. Colby tried to match her fierceness with his own. It was the most intense sex he'd ever had with her. She squeezed his shoulders. She scratched his back. She moaned and cried. Colby could hardly keep his mind on his groin. She grabbed his buttocks to pull him rhythmically between her legs. She moved her hands up to the small of his back, where she continued to tug his thrusts into her, now digging her nails into base of his spine. It crossed his mind that if she dug deep enough, she could paralyze him.

She would not let him slacken his thrusts. She gripped his hips and continued to work him like an implement. Her eyes were closed, and she made liquid sounds in her throat.

He had a vague sense that they'd been arguing a moment ago, but he would not have been able to conjure the reasons for it, even if he'd wanted to.

Frannie gasped and shook under him with her orgasm.

Colby's awareness narrowed and raced toward his groin like a burning fuse, there to set off its little eruption that shut out for a moment everything but Frannie's endearments.

"You fucking prick."

Three

I watch the kid fumbling with the key as he tries to unlock the Forestdale Haul-All Rental Center (Edward Meagre, Prop.). The kid's name is Drew – short for Andrew, I believe. The sky is low and metal-colored. The kid's breath billows in front of him so that he can't see the door handle or the faceplate of the lock. He pokes the door with his key several times before getting it into the keyhole.

The kid doesn't know I am there yet, but he smiles when the key slides home. I know that smile. The power of having his own key and opening the shop by himself. Edward Meagre, Prop. doesn't entrust this task to just anyone. He entrusts it to Drew.

He turns the deadbolt, pulls out the key, and grabs the door handle.

"Good morning," I say.

The kid turns and gives a little jump, as if I am a ninja killer come to punish him. I am not surprised he doesn't recognize me. White people are pretty deficient at recognizing nonwhite faces. But then he does recognize me. "Mr. Harsh," he says. "You startled me."

"I came to return the truck."

He pulls the door open. "Come in, please. Just give me a moment to open up."

He holds the door for a second, but I hang back until

he goes in first. I don't like people following me through doorways.

Inside, he switches on the lights, then walks over to the coffee maker. "Customers don't usually come so early. The rules say you're charged for the whole day on the day of the return. You want to keep it a little longer?"

I don't care about the day's charge. "I'm finished with it."

Drew flicks on the coffee maker and goes over to the counter to switch on the computers. They begin their bubbling and tooting routine while he takes his coat off. "Coffee will be ready in a minute."

"No thanks." I want to be on my way.

"I hope you're not in a hurry," says Drew. "It has to be inspected and then the paperwork written up, and I'm here alone."

"It's out back." I lay the truck key on the counter.

"I just have to print out the inspection form." Drew goes to one of the computers. He looks at the machinery with barely restrained enthusiasm and the wide eyes of a novice. He taps on the keyboard and in a moment I hear the soft screams of the modem as it dials into the Haul-All network. He turns around and goes over to unlock a door labeled "Private" while he is waiting for the connection.

I look around. On the wall behind the counter is a certificate in teal and gold. Edward Meagre, Prop. is certified by Haul-All, Inc. for having completed the company's Supervisory and Human Resources Management Course. *This workplace is managed in accordance with the highest standards of fairness and humane values.*

By force of habit, I have already given the place a casing. Six employees. Drew is the youngest. He has advanced rapidly to a position of responsibility. Soon he will attain the rank of Disillusioned, which is generally the upper limit for sharp, ambitious workers in small- to mid-sized companies, even those managed in accordance with the highest standards of fairness and humane values. "Do you open the place up by yourself every day?"

"Four days a week," he says.

As if I might challenge this, he elaborates. "I'm the senior rental representative."

"Responsible position for somebody in his first job," I say.

"How did you know it's my first job?"

"I know because I remember my first job," I say. "I know what it was like and how it felt, and I recognize it when I see it."

Drew fiddles with the trackball next to his keyboard, then clicks it.

"Are you the only one?" I can tell my questions are making him nervous. Could this strange Asian guy be from a terrorist organization or a doomsday cult? Does he have a plan to take the senior rental representative hostage and attack the Haul-All rental network with nerve gas or green tea?

"The owner is on his way," he says.

"I meant, are you the only senior rental representative."

"Oh. Yeah."

"How many on the staff here? Five? Maybe six?"

Drew looks warily at me. "It will just take a minute for the form to print out."

The best I could get out of this place is six new members. Probably not worth the effort. Still, I like franchises, because they are easy. Franchise owners, as a rule, are not very shrewd. They buy franchises because they think they are safe. I keep my face blank. "How long have you been the senior rental representative?"

Drew looks at the laser printer, where a small green LED has begun to blink. "Two months." He stares at the printer, apparently uncomfortable about looking at me.

"A recent promotion," I say. "I bet the raise came in handy."

The printer whines, and a white page begins to emerge from the output slot.

Drew takes the leading edge of the emerging page in his fingers and begins to pull it from the printer, but the printer is not surrendering except on its own terms. I can tell this kid didn't get a raise with his promotion. I imagine the song and dance that Edward Meagre, Prop. gave him. Sales are down, Drew. Things are pretty tough in the current climate, Drew. Take this promotion now, Drew, and your work will help the sales pick up. Then there will be a big raise for you down the line. Three months. Six months, tops, Drew.

The printer decides to let go of the page. Drew's hand flies up and bangs against the counter.

"Ow." He looks at the back of his hand. There is a faint crease there from the counter edge. He looks at me as if I were the one who hurt him.

"Didn't get a raise with the promotion, did you?" I say.

"I'm not sure that's any of your business, Mr. Harsh." He massages his hand.

"Of course it isn't," I say. "Salary and pay and things like that are highly personal matters, aren't they?"

"Yes, they are."

"You don't talk about your salary, and you don't ask anybody about theirs. It would be rude, wouldn't it?"

He doesn't answer, but with his good hand he pulls a clipboard from under the counter and lays it on the counter. With the heel of his injured hand he presses the clip and pushes the paper under it. He starts toward the door with his clipboard, but I am not through with him.

"You know who invented salary etiquette, don't you?"

He doesn't answer. I feel a cold draft when he opens the door and walks outside. As soon as he is out of sight, I step behind the counter and drop a brochure on the floor there. The logo of the IBOL, a stylized human eye, stares back at me. IBOL. Eyeball. I chose this graphic because I liked the pun, but sometimes I look at it and it seems to speak of the human conscience. Sometimes life arranges itself in ways that have more meaning than we intend.

Then I go to the door marked "Private" and enter the back office. It is a claustrophobic, windowless room with a desk, two chairs, and a couple of file cabinets. There is a copy of *Sensible Supervision* on the desk. I have to chuckle. Nearly every office has a copy of this book. There's nothing in the book that is not readily available to people of decency and common sense, but the publisher has made a fortune among people who think that buying it makes them better managers.

The cabinets are unlocked. There is one drawer for employee files, and Edward Meagre, Prop. has put a label on it: "Employee Files." Probably learned that from *Sensible Supervision*. The drawer is filled with manila folders, most of which have brown labels, except for the six in the front, which have white labels. I deduce that the brown labels are for former employees, of which Forestdale Haul-All Rental Center already has dozens, despite management in accordance with the highest standards of fairness and humane values. Edward Meagre, Prop. is a hair-trigger terminator.

It shouldn't surprise me when a manager uses termination as his first rather than his last disciplinary recourse. It is the most expensive tool available to a manager, but Edward Meagre, Prop. apparently prefers reduced profits to learning the use of any other management techniques, the presence of *Sensible Supervision* notwithstanding. Good management requires no more intelligence than that of an experienced chimpanzee, and while most would-be managers have the intelligence, they lack the chimpanzee's vision.

I pull out the six folders from the front and go through each one until I find the Haul-All Rental Employee Salary Action Form in it. The Haul-All national office supplies the franchise owner with well-designed forms so he can be just like a big company and spend half his time on paperwork. I memorize the names, assess the salaries. The picture is interesting in the way small businesses usually are. Drew works the most hours and he has the most exalted title. And he gets paid the least. Ah, the fairness. Ah, the humanity.

I close the folders and refile them, and I am back in the outer office leaning on the counter when he comes in from the cold. He is carrying his clipboard and cradling his sore hand.

"It was management," I say.

"What?"

"Management," I say. "They're the ones who made up the etiquette about salary. They are the ones who say it's rude to talk about how much money you make. They don't tell your coworkers about your salary because they want to protect your privacy, right?"

He puts his clipboard on the counter. The form has check-marks in all the "yes" boxes. I kept the rental truck clean. He walks around the counter and starts looking for something on a shelf underneath it.

"They don't care about your privacy," I say. "They don't want you talking about your salary because they don't want any of you knowing how much everybody else makes."

He comes up from behind the counter with a rubber stamp in his hand, and the look on his face tells me I am not getting through.

"That kind of information is empowering," I say. "If you know somebody else doing the same job as you is getting paid more, it makes you want to demand more yourself."

"I'm happy with my salary," he mumbles.

"That's great." I smile to keep the observation friendly. "You're a lucky man, if that's the case."

He starts to look a little smug, pleased with having ended the discussion. Or so he thinks.

"Would you be as happy with it if you found out Ike gets twenty-five percent more than you? And he's just an ordinary rental representative. They didn't give him a title, just money."

The smugness evaporates. He knows it is true. I can see it in his eyes. He doesn't even ask me how I know.

"Something to think about," I say. Then I wink at him.

Four

The morning he was to leave, Colby had breakfast with Frannie. He tried to make conversation.

"I cleaned the leaves out of the gutters," he said. It had been a messy job, and he harbored a hidden desire for recognition.

Frannie, drinking coffee from her favorite ceramic mug, looked at him over the rim as if he were the source of an unusual but familiar sound. She said nothing. She put down her coffee mug and lowered her gaze to her corn flakes.

"We won't have any problem with ice dams this winter," said Colby.

Frannie didn't even look up this time.

Colby remembered his thoughts about *King John*. What ever made him think that two people having sex could stop a war?

She did not speak to him for the rest of the meal, and she would not kiss him good-bye when she left for work.

"I'll be back soon," he said.

"Are you sure I'll be here?" she said.

He wondered if it had been a mistake to take the assignment. No, she would get over this. Frannie didn't like change, but she always adjusted to it.

Dennis had supplied Colby with a new sports sedan for the assignment. It had been a long time since Colby had driven anything so comfortable. The driver's seat adjusted ten different ways by means of silent servos that changed the seat's shape and inflated or deflated supportive cushions. One of the adjustments wrapped it closely around the small of his back, making him feel more like he was wearing the car than sitting in it. He had never felt so much in control of an automobile.

He set the handling for TERTIARY ROAD – PAVED and started the car. He put the car in gear, pulled out of the gravel driveway and on to the pavement, then let the car adjust itself to the road condition and the speed limit it received from the GPS satellite. Colby had ridden this stretch of road, from Kimi Pond to Mount Paley, many times, and he often thought of it as a demographic review of modern society. It started in the midst of undeveloped woodland infrequently punctuated with fields and pastures. About twenty miles outside Mount Paley, he began to encounter ambiguous signs of civilization: rusted farm machinery, tumbledown stone fences, cows.

The first house on the route had chickens in the yard, cardboard in several of its windows, a sheet of blue plastic over a section of its roof. There was a gray barn – apparently stripped of its paint by the elements rather than someone making a fashion statement.

This was the land of rural poverty. People here were holding on to their farms by their fingernails. Saddled with a crushing burden of debt, they scraped their living from the actual land. Colby didn't know why they kept at it, except he understood they usually ate pretty well. And most of them just seemed to like being around dirt.

But at ten miles out, the landscape changed completely. The farms and fields and tumble-down houses vanished like dew in the summer sun. They were replaced by the majestic homes of Mount Paley's trophy belt. Here, the landscape was divided entirely into five-acre lots, on each of which stood a three-car garage, four to six ornamental trees, and a two-story house (gray or beige, with butter-colored trim) with at least one natural wood deck, four skylights, three brick chimneys, three palladian windows, and landscaping that looked like it was ordered from an upscale magazine. These were the residences of the region's highest demographic segment, affluent stockholding suburbanites, as a left-leaning demographer labeled them. The ASS class.

The ASS class supplied the region's executives. They ran the financial institutions, the rental companies, the centers of government, the great retail operations of the service economy. Their stock options and bonuses gave them incomes three to ten times what working-class people made. This time of day, their imported luxury sedans were roaring to life to carry their owners to jobs in Mount Paley and even as far south as Forestdale. At the same time they were leaving, the older but well-kept cars and trucks of the service crews were arriving.

Every ASS home supported a phalanx of service workers. Gardeners, house cleaners, handypeople, chimney sweeps, trash removers, baby sitters, dog walkers. The service crews made decent livings traveling from house to house cleaning soap scum from marble bathtubs, dusting glass lampshades, blowing leaves, cleaning swimming pools. The service workers were heavily Asian and Hispanic, and to the extent that he thought about larger, philosophical issues, Colby appreciated that the system could bring cultures together this way.

Colby was wending his way among the ASS homes when, in an unexpectedly ungroomed and heavily wooded section, he came upon what must have been the last ordinary dwelling in the trophy belt. A weather-beaten single-story homestead with several large appliances in the front yard, it appeared never to have been new. It was hardly twenty feet from the edge of the road, and there was no lawn to speak of; the grass had been scraped down to light brown dirt. There was a car of indeterminate age in front of it, but it was old enough to have worn out its tires, because the rubberless wheels sat on cinder blocks. Chained to a massive but blighted oak tree in front of the property, there leaned a large sheet of plywood, on which someone had painted a warning in spray paint of the color commonly known as air-sea-rescue orange:

Nosey people of Mount Paley, go to hell.

Colby could imagine the grizzled homeowner chaining the plywood to the tree and painting the sign, mumbling about citations issued him by town authorities at the behest of his more-civilized neighbors. This close to the interstate highway, he could probably retire comfortably by selling his property to one of the ASSes, but preferred to continue living in poverty, apparently just for the simple joy of offending those around him. His property sat here as defiantly as King John refused to submit to the established order of things, usurping its position from among the ASS homes, disrupting the great chain of being that ran from the lowliest service worker up to the CEO of the largest corporation.

The ASSes in this neighborhood had good reason to be upset about what this homeowner was doing to their property values, but Colby realized he had a grudging admiration for him. What fortitude it must take to put yourself at odds with life as it is supposed to be.

Soon Colby gained the interstate, and as his sports sedan hurtled down the highway, he wondered what he was likely to find at the FOW headquarters. He had always loved the excitement of taking on a new union: planning his moves against the organizer, writing stories for his dear-fellow-employee letters, inciting feverish discussions and animosity.

But Colby had never worked in a union before. He wondered what it would be like. For that matter, why did the FOW object to having its workers unionized? Wasn't that somewhat hypocritical?

Colby wondered if his intuition would give him accurate readings in such a strange atmosphere. He wondered if he would be able to focus on the informal centers of power, find the most influential and charismatic employees, and buy or turn their loyalty. But he knew if he could get the right people on his side, he could hold off a thousand unions. Every society – even the society of a company work force – is feudal, with complicated and arcane systems of fealty, fiefdoms, and overlapping allegiances. Control the aristocracy of a society, and you control the society itself.

The consulting firm's headquarters was in Philadelphia. Colby spent two days there, going over the files on Growth Services and the FOW, getting oriented to all the policy changes that had transpired in the years of his absence, and arranging his first meeting with Harvey Lathrop. It was a strange feeling to be back in the city. So many people, so much noise, so much buying and selling.

After two days he left Philadelphia and booked himself for an extended stay at the Select Suites hotel across the highway from the FOW headquarters in the edge city of Forestdale. He would live in the hotel, on the firm's tab, until the union fight was over. He was not worried about expenses. The firm would pass them through to the FOW.

Colby tended to live stylishly on assignment, and he wondered briefly how the union would account for his expenses
when it was audited by its members or the Department of
Labor or whoever watched over it. But then he realized it
was not a proper question for him to consider. It would be
unethical to treat the FOW differently than he treated any
other client. How they handled his expenses was their
problem.

The room was luxuriously appointed. It was like the
old days when he used to spend so much time on the road
doing prevention and decertification. Bobinga furniture.
Terry cloth robe hanging in the closet. Big screen television.
Queen-sized bed with four pillows. Deep carpeting. He had
forgotten what the pampered life was like.

The night before he was to meet Harvey Lathrop, he
enjoyed a room service dinner. The food was positively
corporate: a juicy chunk of meat and large, tender vege-
tables. Everything was much firmer and tastier than the
organic vegetarian diet he had at home with Frannie.
Frannie insisted on organic food because she said it was the
only way they could make sure they weren't eating geneti-
cally engineered products. Colby had never really been both-
ered by the ancestry of his diet, but he had gone along with
Frannie in the interests of domestic harmony.

When he was finished eating, he looked at the little
tent card on top of the television set to see what might be
on. It was too early in the evening for the soft porno-
graphy advertised on the in-room movie service, and there
didn't seem to be anything else on besides quiz shows. He
thought briefly about going down to the hotel bar, but the
thought of drinking with a bunch of strangers (or worse,
alone) was pretty unappealing. He decided to call Frannie.
After all, it had been a few days, and he hadn't yet called

to let her know he was all right. Surely she was over her anger by now. It was eight o'clock, and he knew she would be home.

But she wasn't home. Colby heard his own voice at the other end when the machine picked up the phone.

"We're not here right now. Please leave your message after the tone."

"It's me," said Colby. "I'll call again tomorrow. Rub Buster behind the ears for me. I miss you."

It wasn't like Frannie to be out in the evening, and Colby was thoughtful as he hung up the telephone. But then he closed his Frannie compartment to clear his mind – a trick he'd learned long ago – and tried to get some sleep before his meeting in the morning.

*   *   *

Colby was ready twenty minutes before he was due for his meeting. He sat in the padded chair by the table and reviewed the Lathrop dossier.

FOW President Harvey Lathrop was not a typical union president, if there is such a thing. He was educated as an economist, and he had written a book, *The Noncooperative Economy,* which had not lit any fires in the world of economic theory, but had done modestly well as a popular explanation of how humanity had arrived at its current situation. Its argument was that corporations had been fundamental to the achievement of modern prosperity but that they had outlived their usefulness.

As a manager, he was an egalitarian. He embraced the working conditions of his employees. He flew coach. He did not allow anyone in his organization to have a reserved parking space. For its staff, the FOW maintained employee benefits identical to those secured by its best current contract.

Colby found himself surprisingly disappointed. He would have preferred to disrespect Harvey Lathrop, but the clipping and the memos in the dossier made him sound like a fair-minded man and a compassionate manager. Despite their rhetoric, Colby knew unions to be authoritarian organizations, capable of exploiting their own workers in the same way they claimed that corporations exploited theirs.

Colby had expected Lathrop would be a punisher. Many times, he had found himself working with clients who were punishers, and it often meant fighting the client as well as the union. Many punishers identify with their organizations in a way that makes them see unionizing as a personal attack. And you can't prevent people from joining a union by punishing them. An organizing drive puts many workers in a strange psychological state that causes them to suspend their normal judgment and abandon their loyalty to their organization. They need sympathy and understanding more than punishment. You can only keep them out of a union by empowering them to see reality for themselves.

The dossier had an article from a union publication: a breathless profile of Lathrop and his philosophy of labor. The photo of Lathrop, an obvious studio portrait Colby had seen many times before, showed a man who was sensitive, self-possessed, and careful in his appearance. His necktie dimple was perfectly centered. Colby felt that was one of the few reliable signs of a civilized man.

Colby reflected on the situation. He'd never worked for a union before. He would need a whole new argument to use in his discussions and his memos. Most of the real work in preventing a union consisted of buying off the right people, but you don't just give a person cash. You have to give him a rationale with it, so he feels right about accepting it. The person you buy needs to be comforted in his decision. Colby always thought of this comfort as "the hand-holding argument."

He looked up from the file. It was ten minutes to nine. He put the papers back into the dossier folder, stuffed it into his calfskin briefcase, checked his necktie dimple in the mirror, and went down to the parking lot. He climbed into his car and started the engine. He let it run for a minute or two. He was just driving across the highway and didn't want to have to shut the car off when there still might be condensation in the engine. He could have walked across the highway, but he felt the way you arrive at a job is important. He didn't want to come straggling in on foot. This was a very strange situation, and he sensed the theatrical aspect of his arrival would be important, if only because of the way it made him feel himself.

It took several minutes to get across the highway, because of the traffic. But he finally got across, parked the car in the FOW headquarters parking lot, climbed out, and walked up to the door. The FOW building was a modest suburban structure: three stories. The headquarters didn't need a large place. It had fewer than one hundred employees.

There was a security man at the reception desk. He was about ten years Colby's junior, with thick black hair and dark, almond-shaped eyes. He was more intense-looking than most security men Colby had known. He was neat and clean, but Colby noticed the collar of his faded khaki shirt was frayed. He had a small black laminated nameplate fastened just above the breast pocket of his shirt. It identified him as Gregg Harsh.

As intense as he looked, however, he was not un-friendly, and he smiled as he offered Colby the registry for signing in.

Colby's last name was common enough, but his first name was quite distinctive, so he used a favorite alias for it.

"Stanley Colby from Mount Paley," the security man read from the registry. "I used to drive a school bus there."

"That's nice," said Colby.

"Do you know a teacher there by the name of Frances Cramer?"

Hearing his wife's name from a stranger raised the hair on the back of Colby's neck, but he gave no sign. "No," he said.

"She always brought the kids out to the bus. I got to chat with her a little. Nice-looking woman. Very down to earth, you know?"

"I'm sure," said Colby.

"Strange you don't know her," said the security man. "I thought everybody in a town that small knew everybody else."

Colby's intuition told him the man knew he was lying about not knowing Frannie.

"I just moved there," said Colby.

"Lousy union the teachers have," said the security man. "Miss Cramer, she told me it was a lot weaker than it needed to be."

Colby's insides froze, but he kept his face relaxed. "Was she active in that union?"

"Don't know," said the security man. "Why do you ask? I thought you said you didn't know her."

"I'm just interested," said Colby. "Unions are a hobby of mine."

"Strange hobby." The security man smiled as if the two
of them had a private joke. He made a brief telephone call.
Colby watched him while he talked on the phone. He kept
the same facial expression, only now he looked like he was
sharing another private joke. Maybe he was just that kind
of person.

The security man looked up from the phone.

"Someone will be here in a moment."

Colby nodded, then looked around the lobby. Why did
Frannie talk with the school bus driver about her union if
she never talked with him about it? Was she hiding something from him?

Of course, Frannie couldn't tell him because she knew
how he would react. He was, after all, a prevention and
decertification consultant, even if he hadn't been active for
a while. Was she really capable of betraying him?

"Mr. Colby?"

Colby turned to see he was being approached by a
young woman with short, unkempt hair the color of an
emergency signal. She wore strange earrings that looked like
obsolete Pentium chips without their heat sinks. She was
dressed in pink denim overalls and red high-top sneakers,
which made her look from a distance like a large piece of
hard candy.

Was Frannie getting involved in her union? He'd agreed
that she had to join, but she had promised to do nothing
more than pay her dues.

As the young woman drew closer, Colby could see that
her overalls retained little of their agrarian heritage. They
were perfectly clean and carefully pressed. Colby realized
with a start that they were a fashion statement of some sort.

"I'm Kathleen." She smiled with even, straight teeth, and
Colby found himself wondering about the FOW's dental plan.

"Dr. Lathrop would have come to meet you himself," she said, "but he's tied up in a meeting."

Colby's mind strayed to Frannie again momentarily. He had to get control of his concentration. A misstep now could endanger the assignment. He decided he would try to call Frannie again tonight, then by an effort of will he closed the Frannie compartment and focused.

Kathleen grabbed his hand and shook it. "Is there anything you need before I show you to his desk?"

Colby just shook his head.

"OK then," she said.

She turned and started back across the lobby. Colby followed her.

She took him through a door in the back of the reception area, and they entered an airplane hangar-sized room that was unlike any workplace Colby had ever visited. There were no interior walls and no partitions. In three directions, he could see the windows to the outside. The air was filled with the soft murmur of conversation mixed with the hum of office equipment. Some effort had gone into the design of the acoustics, because there was none of the echo or reverberation one would expect in a room this size.

Kathleen set off toward the opposite side of the building, skirting a group of three people who appeared to be having a slumber party. The three of them, dressed like aspiring rock musicians, lay on the floor, two supine and chatting at the ceiling, one prone, propped on his elbows and making entries on the keyboard of a laptop computer. Colby realized with surprise that it was a work meeting.

The man with the laptop glanced up at them as they passed. He stopped typing.

"Kathleen."

Kathleen stopped and turned around.

The man stood up. He was wearing black vinyl pants and a tee shirt with no sleeves. He moved toward Kathleen with the posture of a fan hoping for an autograph. "Did you find out about the sour cream yet?"

"There are four employees who are lactose intolerant," she said. "If we can come up with a substitute for them, we can have it."

The man turned to look at his two coworkers on the floor. They looked at one another, then back at him. One of them nodded her head.

"We'll work on it," he said.

"It has to be something that doesn't cost any more than sour cream," said Kathleen. "You know how they are about equity issues."

They continued on and walked past various work-stations, and Colby noticed that no two desks were the same, in either construction or decoration. There were modern, spare-looking desks of Scandinavian provenance, old-fashioned behemoths of dark polished wood, utilitarian specimens of sheet metal and laminate. Colby judged that every employee had the right to choose a desk style.

Even so, the desks showed more uniformity than the people. Colby discerned the typical polyglot grooming of a young work force. Studs, tattoos, and sunglasses were the most ordinary manifestations. He saw polychromatic hair, Hawaiian-style shirts, serapes, baseball caps, and even one woman in riding habit.

Kathleen turned to Colby. "We provide hot chalupas desk side every day. I can't believe how much of my time they take up."

It took him a moment to understand she was explaining the sour cream discussion. He was surprised to realize she was part of the management staff. And what in the world were chalupas?

Kathleen led him through a wilderness of strange workstations and even stranger people, and he would have felt completely lost if he were not able to orient himself by the windows on the horizon. Finally they arrived at a desk that was easily the messiest work space Colby had ever seen.

The desk was littered with photocopies, letters, magazines, software manuals, folders, doubled-over books with broken spines. There were business cards, DVDs, direct-mail flyers, yellow legal pads with curling sheets on top, pencils, pens, three-ring binders, and a road map of Ontario. Virtually every item on the desk had a pink sticky paper on it with a notation in primitive handwriting, as if the place were being catalogued by a museum curator who had failed penmanship.

"Have a seat," said Kathleen. "He'll be with you in a couple minutes."

The only chair was the one behind the desk.

"Where?" said Colby.

But Kathleen was already gone.

Colby sat in the chair and tried to gather his wits from the sensory bombardment he'd just suffered.

"Ah, there you are."

He looked up and saw the human counterpart of the messy desk he was sitting at. He recognized him by the shape of his face, but all the details were unexpected. His suit fit him in the shoulders like collapsed negotiations and in the sleeves like binding arbitration. He needed a haircut, and his necktie looked like he left the knot in it when he took it off. The lenses of his glasses were tinted pink, and Colby realized with a start that they were rose-colored. He'd never seen such a thing before and always assumed it was just a cliché.

Colby rose partway from the seat.

"Don't get up." Lathrop raced over to him and shoved him back down in the chair. He was stronger than he looked.

Colby hit the seat with a grunt.

Lathrop took his right hand and gave it a single shake. "We meet at last." His voice was ironic, and Colby realized he had not expected an ironic man.

"May I get you anything?" said Lathrop.

But before he could answer, Lathrop answered for him. "A cup of tea." He hustled away.

Colby didn't like tea, but he realized it was easier for Lathrop to be doing anything other than talking with Colby about his problem.

Lathrop returned a few moments later carrying two mugs of steaming tea. He handed Colby a mug, then sat on a pile of memos on the desk in front of him. He was near enough that Colby could make out flakes of dandruff at his collar. He gripped the edge of the desk and swung his feet back and forth as he sipped his tea. He looked more like he should be running a software company than a labor union.

"May I set this over there?" Colby gestured with the mug.

Lathrop nodded.

Colby stretched over the desk and set the mug of steaming tea down on a software manual. Then he rolled the chair back from the desk to a more comfortable distance for personal interaction, covering the movement with an elaborate reseating of himself.

Before Colby could start the conversation, they were interrupted by a young woman who appeared behind Lathrop. She was about the same age as the woman who had brought Colby to this desk, but she was dressed for work in an office rather than a circus.

"Excuse me, Dr. Lathrop," she said.

Lathrop turned. "Yes, Lauren. What is it?"

She handed him a clipboard. "This week's chalupas."

Lathrop took the clipboard and signed it. He handed it back to Lauren and waved her away. He turned back to Colby.

"The employees get hot chalupas at their desks every day. It's surprising how much of your time something like that takes up."

"What are chalupas?" said Colby.

"They are some kind of sandwich or something," said Lathrop. "Mexican style."

"You give the employees hot food at their desks?" said Colby.

"Just chalupas," said Lathrop. "They love them. I've never tried one myself."

Colby had never heard of such a thing. This assignment was going to be unlike anything he'd ever done before.

"They tell me you think your organization is the object of an organizing effort," said Colby.

Lathrop's expression clouded. "I take it you find this amusing."

"I didn't say that," said Colby.

"We had better acknowledge our history, Mr. Colby," said Lathrop. "Otherwise, it will come out unexpectedly and bite us."

"Please call me Cole, Dr. Lathrop."

"Would that make you feel more comfortable?" said Lathrop.

"We'll probably have to work fairly closely together," said Colby.

"Fine," said Lathrop.

The two sat in an uncomfortable silence for a moment.

Colby realized that Lathrop's embarrassment was a major component of the cloud that hung between them.

"You should call me Harv," said Lathrop at last.

Colby kept himself from sighing with relief. Getting on a first-name basis with his former adversary seemed a major step. He was glad it was behind him.

Lathrop was obviously still embarrassed, but he was too big a man to allow embarrassment to get in the way of business. "You have to understand our position here, Cole." He sipped his tea, then continued. "We have a fiduciary responsibility to our members. We owe them the most efficient possible use of our operating resources, which come from them in the form of dues."

Colby had always thought of labor unions as businesses, but he had never thought about the customer service aspect before. Of course they would have to be as responsive to their members as any business was to its customers. He was beginning to uncover the concept of the new philosophy he needed, so he pushed Lathrop for more insight.

"Surely your members couldn't object to the headquarters employees belonging to their union?" he said.

Lathrop shook his head emphatically. "The Department of Labor will not allow a union's employees to belong to the union itself. We would be negotiating the employment contract with ourselves, you see."

Of course. If the employees at this site joined the FOW,

it would be no better than a company union, and even Colby recognized the company union as a discredited tool for fighting unionization.

"So what are we to do, then?" continued Lathrop. "We cannot cede representation of our employees to outsiders. We're up against our fiduciary responsibility again."

There was much more here than a comic situation. The interests of the union's members was an angle he had not thought of. The phrasing of his hand-holding argument began to form in his head. *The members of the FOW rely on you to protect their interests. They want their union to provide the services it is supposed to provide, not get mired in contract negotiations, formal work procedures, and excessive pay scales.*

"Has this union called you?" he said to Lathrop.

"No."

"How do you know it's trying to organize you?"

"One of my vice presidents found this in the trash." Lathrop pulled a crumpled flyer from his jacket pocket and handed it to Colby.

Colby found a bare spot on the desk and smoothed the flyer out. It had a stylized human eye on it. Under the eye was the acronym IBOL, and Colby realized the acronym was meant to be pronounced. It was actually rather clever. When he looked up at Lathrop again, he saw his client was not looking at him.

Lathrop had his head down, and his hand grasped his forehead, covering his eyes.

Colby realized the man didn't know he was being looked at. He looked back down at the brochure again, embarrassed, then said something to give Lathrop a chance to collect himself.

"I like the FOW's brochures better."

He looked up at him again. Lathrop had collected himself enough to smile, but the strain showed on his face.

"I've tried to treat them like family, Cole," he said. "I don't know why they would do this to me."

Colby started to tell him not to take it personally, which is what he usually told clients in this situation, but he realized it would sound hollow, maybe even patronizing.

"Tell me, Harv, are you aware of any of your employees signing union membership cards?"

"No."

"You haven't identified a single one?" said Colby.

Lathrop said nothing for what seemed several moments. Then he set down his tea. "I'd have fired anybody who signed one."

Five

I am a combined receptionist and security guard for the FOW. My assignment is geographical rather than functional. I work at the security desk in the front lobby. *What* I do is pretty variable. I have no actual job description. The FOW wants no limitations on what employees can be used for. That is not to say it is a bad place to work. They bring us warm chalupas every day, and there is a rumor they may be adding sour cream to them soon.

It matters to me very little whether a site is a good place to work or a bad place to work. I am here to start a union for the people who work here.

I have made one contact so far, but the young man seemed more interested in a date with me than in joining the union. I thought it best not to lead him on. If I am to date anyone in this place, it must be someone who can be useful to me – someone who enjoys respect and influence. And I think that person is the union's Vice President of Operations. She has just stopped here at my reception desk on her way out the door. She removes a set of keys from the pocket of her pink overalls and speaks to me.

"Gregg, I'm taking a late lunch. Anything from Flashburger?"

The hardware hanging from her ear lobes must be

heavy, because the flesh looks as if it has begun to stretch a little from the weight of it.

I wonder if I can turn this offer to advantage.

"Thanks, Kathleen, but I was just thinking about asking Ken to take over for me so I can go myself."

"Hey, why don't you come with me!" she says.

Such an invitation from a woman to a man inevitably inspires speculation, which she hurries to dispel with an explanation. "I hate to eat alone."

"Me too." I lie to her, as I lie to everyone here.

She resettles the strap of her shoulder bag, which is red canvas and matches her high-top sneakers.

I call Ken on the phone and ask him to come out and take over for me. "I'll cover for you this Saturday," I promise.

"You're on," says Ken. "Give me five minutes."

"He's going to be a couple minutes," I say to Kathleen. "I'll meet you in the parking lot."

"Massive." She departs in a rattle of keys.

I don't know what "massive" means in this context, but I assume it is simply some sort of affirmation.

Most of the staff here were hired as employees of the union, but a few – all executives, like Kathleen – are officers of the FOW who are here on permanent or temporary assignment. Kathleen was apparently elected by a constituency of clerks to participate in managing their union. It is an interesting situation, really. She is a worker put into the role of manager. The young man who was my first contact told me she was a lover of Harvey Lathrop's. I am going to learn a great deal at lunch.

I am now alone in the lobby. I call up a document on my computer screen. It consists of a single line of text.

Thread the rude eye of rebellion.

I smile, thinking of the frustration this message will cause. Shakespeare, of course, said "unthread the rude eye of rebellion," but my change makes it sound more threatening. I look around. Ken will not arrive for a few minutes. I open my network browser and route the document to a site called The Faceless Fax. It will let me send a fax to any fax receiver in the world with no originating information. I suppose eventually a first-rate technician could find an identifier for this machine on the server of The Faceless Fax, but the site guarantees that such an investigation will take months, and by that time I will be long gone from this place. I tap in the fax number for Stillman Colby's consulting firm and click the SEND button. It only takes a second for the site's software to report a successful transmission.

Stanley Colby. What a joke. These people are pretty inept if they think I didn't expect them to bring the famous Stillman Colby out of retirement for this fight.

"Unthread the rude eye of rebellion" is from *King John,* which is more appropriate than any of Colby's colleagues will understand. I enjoy the vision of the firm's specialists puzzling over it. I had thought of writing "the eyeball of rebellion," but that would have made it too easy. This way, one of them will eventually make the connection between eye and IBOL, and they will think they have solved it. I log off the site, then open the browser's history file and delete its URL, and then delete it again from Trash.

When I get to the parking lot, there is a red sport utility vehicle at the curb, honking its horn. The car's paint is about the same color as Kathleen's hair. I go over and climb in. The moment I pull the door shut, the car jumps away from the curb with a squeal.

The car is well appointed, with leather upholstery and cupholders protruding from more places than I can count. Rock music emanates from speakers artfully hidden throughout the cabin. I look around inside and marvel at the luxury.

Kathleen sees me examining everything. "My one serious indulgence," she says.

Flashburger is only fifteen minutes away, but the drive feels like hours. Kathleen is the most irritating driver I have ever encountered. The car is always either speeding up or slowing down. She drives with the ardor of a child using crayons for the first time: staying more or less inside the lines but daubing at one side or the other of her travel lane in an apparent effort to cover as much of the pavement as possible. Despite the risk involved in taking her attention from the road, I ask her about the visitor she escorted earlier today.

"He seems to be a consultant." She has just accelerated to highway speed on this suburban street and now steps on the brake to slow the car before it strikes a Federal Express van parked in front of us. I am thrown forward in the seat, and I thank providence for the shoulder harness. Irritation turns to fear, however, as it becomes apparent we will not stop in time. But Kathleen swerves the car around the van and starts to accelerate again, thrusting me back into the seat.

"Any idea who he was?" I manage.

"He was dressed like a man in that fashion magazine, you know?" She turns to look at me and, as if her hands and head are connected by invisible wires, pulls the steering wheel in the same direction. The car has appreciable body roll, and my heart jumps into my throat as I feel it starting to tip over toward my side.

"*GQ*?" My voice squeaks when I try to use it.

"That's the one." She turns back to face the road, and the car rights itself. "He looked kind of stodgy, but he was stodgy in a massive way. No style, for sure, but his clothes were really well cut. I diagnose him for an ASS."

Kathleen is one who notices clothes. I only have to look at her pink denim overalls and fire-engine red hair to understand she has a well-developed sense of fashion. I feel my body rising from the seat and straining against the harness again as the car comes to an abrupt halt.

"Damn red light," she says. "I can never make this one. Dark suit with a stripe you could barely see. Why would you have a stripe if you have to get close to see it?" She looks at me. I am not wearing a suit.

I recover my self-possession. I wonder how soon Kathleen will know "Stanley" Colby is here to stop me.

Flashburger is crowded with customers when we arrive, but the staff work with good-humored deliberation, and the line of customers is moving quickly.

Kathleen orders two double cheeseburgers, one large serving of french fries, a deep-fried apple pie, and a soda. I order a salad, since I have already eaten once today.

When I hand him the money, I can see in the eyes of the counter man, Jack, that he recognizes me. But he does me the courtesy of not showing it, and I am spared the awkwardness of arousing Kathleen's curiosity.

"I like the food here," Kathleen says as we sit down to eat. "It's really fluent, you know?"

"Fluent?"

"Yeah."

She is praising the food. Why doesn't she simply say it is good? This, I realize, is part of what makes Kathleen seem so real compared to the other union executives. She uses the language idiosyncratically, and this seems to be a way of staying in touch with her roots. The other executives at this union seem more like Stillman Colby than like the office workers they are supposed to be representing. As soon as they win election to the executive ranks, they start dressing and talking like any other manager. I wonder if Kathleen understands how seriously she limits her prospects for "advancement" by her style of dress and her refusal to master their phrasebook.

I tear the corner from my salad dressing packet. "This place is about to go union."

"Really?" She sips from her soda. "Good for them. How did you hear about it?"

"I read about it in the newspaper," I say. I know of no newspaper that would publish such a report, of course, but I don't want to tell her how I really know.

She turns to look at the five people behind the counter, most of whom are sweating and all of whom are working like galley slaves. She turns back and eats a french fry. "A few work rules will make their lives better."

I realize that Kathleen is destined to struggle with conflicting loyalties. She really believes in unionization, but her responsibilities as an executive will demand that she fight it at the FOW headquarters.

I decide to test her. "I hope the union doesn't ruin things."

She looks at me seriously. "What do you mean?"

"You know how it is with union shops," I say. "They try to keep the work standards low, and when they are dissatisfied, they sit down on the job."

"What union shop do you belong to, Gregg?"

"None." I must sound silly, and I cannot help but laugh. It pleases her. "You have a felicific laugh, Gregg."

I have never heard this word before, but I cannot lose conversational momentum to ask about it. "I try not to wear it out," I say.

We chew in silence for a moment.

"Do you know what assembly-line workers used to call their work?" she says.

"Are we talking about assembly-line workers?"

"This country used to have a lot of factories that used assembly lines," she says, as if that answers my question. "A lot of people made their livings on assembly lines before the jobs all went overseas."

I take a bite of my salad, as if I am not interested.

" 'Fighting the line,' " she says. "Fifty years ago, if you worked on an assembly line in an automobile factory, your job might be to install a dashboard or connect an exhaust system. You did the same thing on each car as it came past your work station."

"Sounds boring," I say.

"There are worse things than boredom," she says.

"I guess you've never been a security guard," I say.

She ignores my joke. "You master an assembly line job quickly. But soon, usually within a few days, certainly within a few weeks, you drift into a mental state unlike anything else you've ever felt before. It's like being dazed and tense at the same time."

I wonder where Kathleen came by her knowledge of assembly lines.

"Factory work is mostly automated now," she says. "But there is still a lot of assembly by workers that goes on in Asia and Latin America: computers, electronics, small appliances."

I realize Kathleen has probably lived abroad and worked on one of these assembly lines herself.

"An assembly line turns a worker into a mechanical process," she says, "and there's a part of her that refuses to accept it. So she rebels. Not by breaking things or attacking the boss or anything like that. She can't risk losing this job that turns her into a mechanical process. In the choice between being a mechanical process with well-fed children and being a rebel against authority with a starving family, most people choose the mechanical gig.

"So the worker rebels in the only way possible. She works at her own pace. Now she can't work slower than the line, because the line never slows down. So if she is going to get control, she has to work faster.

"She works faster and installs her controller module before the next disc player has rolled into position. And that way, she scores a little victory against the line and gains momentary control of her life. She even gets to rest for a moment before the next unit arrives at her workstation."

"Good for her," I say.

"Yeah. Except that everybody else does it, too. You can't help it. You have to work faster. It is your only chance at being human."

I nod and put my plastic fork down. I am fascinated to see where she is going with this.

"When everybody works faster, everybody gets a little break between units. But every factory employs a reptile known as a time-and-motion specialist, whose job it is to send a report to management whenever worker idleness reaches the point of being noticeable. There is nothing management hates worse than idle workers, so when management gets this reptile's report, it increases the speed of the line. And the cycle starts again."

I have a picture in my mind of Kathleen wearing a

paper suit and a hair net, trying to assemble disc players fast enough to gain a little control over her life.

"On an assembly line," she says, "the more you control your work, the less control you have over it. The harder you work to keep your humanity, the less human you become."

We are silent for a moment over our plastic trays of fast food.

"Why are you telling me this?" I say.

She picks up her cheeseburger again, and raises it toward her mouth. "It is by way of explaining that sometimes the only way to stand up for yourself is to sit down."

Six

Back in his hotel room, Colby allowed himself to think again about the security guard. What was his name? Gregg something. Gregg Harsh. The man said he knew Frannie, and that she complained about that teachers' union she belonged to. She had never complained about it at home. That was strange. Was she hiding something from him? Was she thinking about becoming an activist again? She had promised him when he left the business that she was out of it for good as well. But Colby always suspected she had a compulsion to organize. She wouldn't be wildcatting, would she?

Colby picked up the phone and dialed his house. The answering machine played its greeting in his own voice. He waited for it to finish. When the beep sounded, he called urgently into the phone.

"Frannie? Frannie, would you pick up! I need to talk to you. It's important. Frannie?"

There was a clicking on the line, followed by Frannie's voice.

"What is it, Still?"

Colby's intuition told him that he should not start talking about his concerns right away. He barely had her on the phone. He had to be careful if he was going to keep her there. "I'll be home soon," he said. Too late, he realized how stupid it sounded.

"You said there was something important." Her voice was businesslike. Frannie had always been task-oriented.

"I needed to know you were all right," he said. "You didn't answer the last time I called. I was afraid something had happened to you."

"I'm fine."

She did not sound hostile. But she wasn't very forthcoming, either.

"Is everything all right at school?" said Colby.

"Why wouldn't it be?"

"I met a man here who says something is going on there."

"What man?"

Colby wished she had asked first about the goings-on rather than the man reporting them.

"His name is Gregg Harsh," said Colby. "Do you know him?"

Frannie said nothing. There was a clicking sound somewhere in the room, and Colby could hear the hotel's ventilation system give out a groaning sigh, then settle into a soft, strained hum. A cold breeze touched his cheek.

"Frannie?"

"No," she said. "No. I don't know him. Who is he?"

* * *

Fifteen years before, during the Growth Services fight against the FOW, Colby's brother Hank had been in an automobile accident, was critically injured, and lay in the hospital in a coma. Colby had been too much in the thick of the job to get away, but he called every day to ask his parents how his brother was.

Dennis had told Colby he could take some time off.

"You ought to be there, Cole," said Dennis. "He's your brother."

"We'll lose if I leave now," said Colby. "I'm the only one who knows the case well enough to keep the pressure on."

"What about your parents?"

"My being there isn't going to help them," said Colby. "I'm not a surgeon. What can I do?"

Dennis just shook his head. "Sometimes I don't get you, Cole."

"What separates the professional from the tyro," said Colby, "is the ability to compartmentalize. This may be our only chance to stop this union. That's the compartment I'm in right now. I'll stay here until the job's done."

Colby, of course, turned out to be right. The client won the fight against the FOW, and it had been the great triumph of Colby's career, responsible for his fame as a union buster and for his promotion to partner. Hank came out of his coma after a week, and over the course of a year made an apparently full recovery. It was a lesson Colby had never forgotten. Don't let anything distract you from the job at hand.

As he prepared to start work the next morning, Colby opened a consultant compartment and stepped into it. The compartment he had left, which contained Frannie, his cabin, and his dog Buster, would have to remain closed until the FOW matter was settled. There was nothing he could do in that compartment until he was finished here, so why think about it?

Harvey Lathrop had asked Kathleen to work with

him. She was the young woman who had come out to the lobby to meet him when he first arrived. She turned out to be the union's Vice President of Operations, which surprised Colby. Among all the vice presidents Colby had met, she was the first who had neglected to use her title when she introduced herself. Her demeanor, while confident and self-possessed, made her seem more like an office worker than an executive. But then, holding an elective office in the union meant that she *was* an office worker in some sense. She had to be if she were to be a member of the union. Colby felt like he had stepped through the looking glass into a world where the managers were workers and the workers were ... what?

It crossed Colby's mind that Lathrop had assigned Kathleen to him so she could spy on him, but he dismissed that thought when he saw how surly she was. If she were spying, she would have put on an act of some sort. But Kathleen plainly opposed Colby's work. She never complained out loud, but she moved slower than she should have, and she did nothing he did not directly tell her to do.

Colby realized he would have to win her over first. He could not run this campaign with a viper in his nest. And his intuition told him that if he did win her over, it would be very meaningful, because she seemed widely liked.

As always, Colby would work by the book and make a show of mobilizing the union's supervisors against IBOL. But while he did all that in the open, he would also pursue another, more covert strategy: he would find the key workers at the site and harden them against the organizing effort through personal counseling. This counseling might involve promotions, payments, and – if need be – intimidation. With the support of Harvey Lathrop, he would be in a position to make the workers' lives rewarding or miserable. Playing to those possibilities was the essence of stopping IBOL in its tracks.

He needed privacy for his counseling sessions. So the first order of business was to establish an office. Since the only room at the FOW headquarters was a conference room, Colby booked a small office in the business services department of the Select Suites Hotel where he was living. The office had everything he needed: two rooms with a desk in each one, two telephones, and two chairs in each room. Colby was satisfied. He even thought that taking the employees off site for their meetings with him would have a salutary effect. He and Kathleen were moved in by the end of his second day on the job.

His second order of business was to get a budget to be used for buying off the influential employees as he identified them.

He met with Lathrop the day after he was moved into his new office. He came over to the FOW building and found a chair to place in front of Lathrop's desk. The two of them spoke over the piles of debris that seemed to give the union president so much comfort.

"What budget?" said Lathrop. "I thought I was simply to pay your firm's retainer."

"Yes," said Colby. "But I need resources to conduct my work. This kind of thing works best if there is a reserve for subornation fees."

"My operating funds are all committed," said Lathrop. "I don't have any money for – what did you call them?"

"Subornation fees."

"You're saying I have to buy off my own employees?" said Lathrop. "Is this how you used to beat me in elections?"

"I guess we're going to learn a lot about each other's methods," said Colby. "This is the most efficient way to do it, and it's the way it's always been done."

"I thought as much," said Lathrop sullenly.

They sat across from each other in tense silence.

"Harv," said Colby at last, using his most friendly tone, "I'm sure you too did things that weren't on the up and up when you were fighting me."

"I thought you were supposed to hold some sort of rally and build morale."

Colby did not let his smirk show on his face. So many people still believed in fairy tales.

"We should convince them that the best way to keep good working conditions and a good relationship with management is to keep the union out," said Lathrop.

Colby leaned back in the chair. "Harv, have you ever heard of Boston City Hospital?"

"No."

"It doesn't exist anymore. Now it's just part of Boston Medical Center. But back when it was a municipal hospital, Boston City Hospital was one of the first hospitals in the country with a house officers' union."

"House officers?"

"Interns and residents," said Colby.

"You mean the doctors were unionized?" said Lathrop.

"Oh yes," said Colby. "And not only were they unionized, but they went on strike every time their contract ran out. Every time. 'We can't continue working a hundred hours a week,' they said. 'We're dead on our feet. We make mistakes ordering treatment. Patient care suffers. It's unsafe for us to work so many hours.' And they went on strike to get shorter hours and safer conditions."

"What did the hospital do?"

"What could they do?" said Colby. "The only way to give them shorter hours was to hire more house officers, and there weren't enough doctors to do that. So they offered them a raise."

"Did it work?" said Lathrop.

"Not at first," said Colby. "They were striking for shorter hours and safer working conditions, not a pay raise. But at every negotiating session, the hospital would offer a little more salary, and its p.r. people would release stories about how patients were suffering and going untreated because of the strike. It usually took them about three weeks to settle, but in the end the doctors always called off the strike for a pay increase of twenty-five to thirty percent."

"What's the point of this story?" said Lathrop.

"You want to build morale, promise them better working conditions, and so on, but in the end you'll always have to buy them off. It works for doctors. It works for anybody."

Lathrop sat silently for a long time.

"I won't spend the money unless it's absolutely necessary," said Colby.

Lathrop didn't look up, but spoke to the piles of debris on his desk. "How much do you need?"

* * *

Colby knew that, in the end, stopping a union means bribing and bullying the right people. But he also knew that bribing and bullying are illegal, so he had to simultaneously run a legitimate campaign. He had to hold the meeting Harvey Lathrop wanted: the meeting that would bring the supervisors together and invest them with the spirit of the campaign.

Colby insisted that Lathrop himself run the supervisors' meeting. He wrote a script for him. Colby, still wanting to preserve his anonymity, did not want to be introduced or even acknowledged to the supervisors.

Colby asked Kathleen to book the second-floor conference room and arrange to have a security guard at the door. This was mostly for show, to send a subtle signal to the organization that he was capable of tracking employee movements. Then he asked Kathleen to notify the supervisors of the meeting and to bring a list of them so she could check off their names as they arrived.

Colby arrived at the conference room to find Kathleen standing at the door dressed in yellow overalls and green high-topped sneakers. She was wearing strange earrings again, and when Colby looked at them closely, he noticed they were polished keys – not jewelry meant to resemble keys but actual keys.

The clear plastic panel next to the conference room door bore a reservation notice identifying his meeting. "Where's the security guard?" he said.

"Oh." Kathleen did not hide her surliness. "I forgot about that."

It occurred to Colby that she would be a liability at this meeting. He abandoned his plan to have her check off the names of the supervisors as they arrived. And he was pleased to have a ready-made excuse to get rid of her. "Could you go find one and bring him?"

Kathleen nodded and left.

Colby looked at the glass wall of the conference room. He went inside and pulled the curtains closed. He did not want to advertise this meeting to anyone walking past in the hallway. Then he sat down to wait for everyone. There would be a dozen supervisors. He did not have to bring in supervisors from other locations, because the organizing effort seemed to be limited to headquarters. If it was successful, IBOL would probably try to branch out and unionize the employees at the FOW's locals, but it obviously lacked the people to organize more than one site at a time.

Colby had expected Lathrop to wait until all the supervisors had arrived before making his entrance. Any CEO should know the importance of theatrics – pomp and circumstance. Employees respond to it. They like to think their CEO is important.

But Lathrop showed up first. He entered smiling, eyes bright behind his pink lenses, and took a seat at the round conference table. Colby greeted him and acceded to his suggestion that he sit beside him.

The earliest supervisors – three of them – did not take their seats but came right over and lined up before Lathrop. As orderly as peasants seeking the lord's touch to cure their scrofula, they approached him one at a time. Lathrop chatted with them as they came, beginning the conversation each time with a specific question, such as "Did your boy make the team?" or "Did you get the lease?"

Colby had never met a CEO who knew more about the details of his managers' lives. Some of the conversations were quite personal. Lathrop doled out advice on marriage and family, guidance on financial matters, encouragement in hobbies. Once or twice he took money from his pocket and passed it unobtrusively to his interlocutor. Colby looked the other way when this happened. It was like sitting next to an old-time ward heeler, and it was embarrassing.

More supervisors got into line as they entered. If Colby hadn't known better, he would have thought he was listening in each case to a brother with a younger sibling. There was a great deal of banter, and each of these hurried conversations seemed to end with a pat on the shoulder or a squeeze of the arm.

As Colby watched Lathrop speak with each supervisor, he realized one of the reasons the man wanted to have this meeting was so Colby could see how close he was to his people. Colby smiled inwardly. Eventually perhaps, he would feel sufficiently at ease with Lathrop to tell him how little difference any of that made. In the course of his career, Colby had seen union organizing fights split up lifelong relationships. He had seen brothers turn against brothers and wives against husbands. He had even known an organizer who unionized his own father's company. This was not about loyalty and affection. It was about power and control.

When Colby looked toward the doorway, he saw the last few supervisors come in and seat themselves, too late to engage Lathrop in conversation before the meeting. People sat around the table and chatted softly and amiably. Something made Colby feel vaguely uneasy. He could not put his finger on it.

Lathrop finished up with his group of supplicants, who seated themselves around the table with the others. When Colby saw that the dozen seats were filled, he leaned down to his companion. "You're on, Harv."

Lathrop nodded. As Colby went over to close the conference room door, the union president stood up. He removed his glasses, looked around the room, then put them back on again.

Colby slipped quietly back into his seat at the table.

"Ladies and gentlemen," said Lathrop, "they are trying to take our union away from us."

Colby could feel the admiration and affection these

employees had for this man, and he was pleased Lathrop was following the script he had written for him. This would be a good assignment. He had good people to work with.

"We have found evidence that a union is attempting to organize our staff." Lathrop paused while the murmur went around the room.

"We believe in unions here, of course," said Lathrop. "We couldn't very well do this work if we didn't."

Lathrop paused, and a soft chuckle passed through the crowd. Lathrop gazed across the room, sharing the irony with his people. The laughter died away.

"But I don't have to tell you," continued Lathrop, "that we have a responsibility to our members, a responsibility we take most seriously." He stopped again and looked around the table, stopping at each face long enough to make a connection.

Colby could see that these people were loyal to their boss. They were loyal in the best way possible, which is to say they identified their own interests with his.

But the silence became uncomfortable, and Colby wondered what his client was doing. Was this a pause for dramatic effect? Was he planning some departure from the script?

Lathrop looked directly at Colby, then continued. "Fortunately, we have the assistance of a human resources consulting firm in formulating our strategy. I'd like to introduce Stillman Colby, a prevention and decertification specialist. He will give you an idea of what to expect. I want you to give him your complete cooperation until we have this fight won."

Colby didn't know whether to feel anger that Lathrop had gone against their agreement or fear at having to address all these people when he had nothing prepared. But he willed his face into a mask and stood up.

"We're depending on you." Lathrop shook hands with him and sat down again.

Colby wondered why Lathrop had done this to him. But he didn't have long to think about it, for a dozen faces were staring at him expectantly, and he had to tell them something useful that would not hamper his own plans. He was barely aware of the door opening across the room and Kathleen slipping in to seat herself at the table.

"Welcome to the fight of your lives," said Colby.

He looked down at the table, in case he could see the script he'd written for Lathrop. But the president had closed a manila folder on the script and sat with his hands folded on it.

"Most of you have only theoretical experience of union organizing," said Colby. "While you do the union's day-to-day business, you never have much contact with organizing until it is over.

"But it is time for you to learn how organizing is done, because you must understand what is being done to your workplace. Organizing is not always pretty, ladies and gentlemen. I'm sure you're aware that in many ways, a labor union is a business. It has products – organizing and negotiating – and it has customers, its members.

"Like any other business, you conduct marketing campaigns. The FOW itself does this when it sends organizers out to companies for membership drives. Obviously, being in the business does not confer any protection on you from your competitors. The International Brotherhood of Labor, your competitor, has targeted your employees as an untapped market. It has sent a sales agent to try to convince

your employees to buy. This sales agent has not yet identified himself. He will try to ingratiate himself with your
people before he gives them his pitch. Some of them will
find him persuasive, and they will buy what he is selling.
When they buy, IBOL will then engage them to sell their
friends and coworkers." Colby stopped his anti-union
argument here. He had to walk a fine line.

"The FOW is already very generous with employee
benefits and compensation. It's one of the best in your
industry." Colby looked at Lathrop for confirmation.

Lathrop did not confirm it, but simply gazed blandly
back at him.

He looked around the room to see if there were any
challenges. There were none, so he continued. "So you see,
the employees here have little to gain from a union." Colby
paused to let them digest this before he went on to the
supervisors' role in the coming struggle.

"If FOW employees have nothing to gain, they do have
something to lose. They will have to pay union dues, and
for many of them it will not be an insignificant part of their
personal budgets." Colby paused. What else did they have
to lose? He looked around at the expectant faces. His intuition came to his aid. "If this site becomes unionized, some
employee benefits will be lost because management will be
too busy responding to union demands to administer them
properly. You can tell your employees they will lose their
chalupas first."

Some of the faces looked disappointed.

"Just remember," said Colby, "that whatever the
employees lose, you lose as well." He looked around the
room to make sure he had their attention. They were all
watching him closely. "But, in fact, you have a lot more to
lose than the employees do.

"If the union secures representation for the employees of this site, many of you will lose your jobs."

Colby stopped, and he heard a gasp here and there.

"I can't tell you how many or who it will be," he said. Now it was time to move it out of the realm of overt threat. "In every election I've witnessed in which the union has won, some percentage of the supervisors have lost their jobs. In every election I've witnessed in which the union lost, none of them has."

Colby's intuition told him that he had them. Before Colby had begun reading Shakespeare, he'd read Boswell's *Life of Johnson,* and he remembered now something that Johnson had supposedly said. "Depend upon it, sir, when a man knows he is to be hanged in a fortnight, it concentrates his mind wonderfully."

Colby looked around. They were still staring at him expectantly, perhaps hoping for some hints on how to make certain of holding on to their jobs and their chalupas. No one stirred. He looked down at Lathrop, who nodded, although he was plainly uncomfortable.

"I have an office in the hotel across the street," said Colby. "If you have any questions, please don't hesitate to come and ask me. If you hear of any of your people joining the union, or being approached about joining the union, please tell me." Colby looked down at Lathrop again. Two can play this game. "Dr. Lathrop has authorized me to offer a small bonus to anyone who reports to me on activity that proves to be part of the union organizing effort." He smiled at Lathrop, and Lathrop nodded.

"I look forward to working with you," said Colby.

He heard hands clapping, and he looked up to see one of the supervisors offering polite applause. Others followed suit, and soon the room was filled with the sound of applause. Colby was surprised at how gratified he felt. He smiled in spite of himself and basked in the noise. He gazed around the room, and with the pressure off he began to understand the source of the unease he had felt when he watched the supervisors entering. They were all young people. He doubted there was a single person over thirty-five here besides himself and Lathrop. Colby looked down at Lathrop. The CEO wasn't much over forty himself. Colby was the oldest person in the room.

Colby gestured for Lathrop to stand beside him. It was a good opportunity to demonstrate again that he had the support of the site's top man. Lathrop stood beside him and nodded to the supervisors.

Colby could not keep himself from smiling. There was nothing that made him feel better than being in control. The door opened, and Colby looked over to see who was entering. The applause continued, and the security guard Gregg Harsh slipped into the room. Harsh just stood next to the door and smiled directly at Colby.

Seven

It is near quitting time, and although her bright red sport utility vehicle is in the company parking lot, I have not seen Kathleen since the meeting this morning. I wonder if I should try to find her home telephone number, but I do not know what I would say if I got her on the phone.

People have begun to depart for the day. It is never a big rush at the FOW headquarters. There is no regimentation here. People leave in small clots of two or three, chatting exhaustedly as they head out of the building toward their waiting personal lives. As more and more of them exit the double doors in front of my reception desk, a tide of stillness rises from the floor until the quiet seems to be waist deep. I look toward the sunset through the tinted windows. I swivel my chair and stare at the door to the work area, even though I know Kathleen will not be coming through it. I am moody, and it is a strange feeling for me. Perhaps I shall take the night off. Maybe take a bottle of something back to my room.

"Hi, Gregg."

I swivel back to my desk and find Kathleen standing before me in denim overalls of bright yellow and forest-green high-top sneakers. She drops her shoulder bag on to my desk. She still has house keys dangling from her ear lobes. The creativity she applies to the making of cheap

jewelry is remarkable. I notice my feeling of moodiness has
evaporated.

"Where did you go after that meeting?" I say.

"I'm working across the street." She jerks her thumb
over her shoulder toward the hotel.

"With Colby?"

She nods. "Harv's had me working with him since
yesterday. He's set himself up at the hotel."

"Will you be there long?"

"Why? Do you miss me?" She is chuckling, as if the
idea is absurd.

But I see an opportunity to ingratiate myself. "Yes," I
say.

She stops chuckling and looks at me quizzically. Then
her face relaxes with an apparent understanding. "It takes
the new guy a while to make friends, I guess."

"I enjoyed our lunch yesterday," I say.

She raises an eyebrow, and her look is not uninviting.
"You aren't getting personal on me, are you, Gregg?"

I must let this seem to happen naturally. I must not
push it. "I don't make friends easily."

She makes a friendly smile, then strains to hoist the
strap of her bag on to her shoulder again. She turns to head
off toward the work area.

I try to think of what I can say to get her to remain
here. What will seem natural and friendly? I decide to try
her principal weakness. I speak to her retreating back.

"If you don't have plans, I would be pleased to treat
you to dinner at Flashburger."

She stops and turns to look back at me. I can almost
see the cheeseburgers and fries dancing in her eyes. "That
would be massive."

* * *

Somehow, we survive the trip to Flashburger in her car.

I generally prefer to eat alone, but I would find eating with Kathleen to be a diversion even if she weren't necessary to my plans. Her conversation is engaging, she is pleasant to look at, and her improvised jewelry is both stylish and amusing. And she eats with such relish that it is enjoyable to watch her.

"What are you doing for Colby?" I say between bites of a grilled chicken sandwich.

"He just needs somebody to get things done for him, somebody who knows the organization." She dabs with a napkin at a bit of special sauce on the corner of her lip.

"Is it interesting work?"

"It makes me uncomfortable."

Kathleen is not one to share her feelings with those below her, and I can tell that *uncomfortable* is understating it.

"I'm a union activist," she says. "I don't like working to stop a union."

For a moment, neither of us speaks. Perhaps she feels she has said too much. I want to put her at ease. "What's Colby like to work with?"

She shrugs. "He wanted to do this all undercover, but Harv surprised him by introducing him at the employee meeting yesterday. So that was good."

"No. Really?"

"Veracious," she says.

It is a word I have not heard before, but I can guess at its meaning.

"Now we have to go out to some truck stop on the interstate tomorrow," she says. "They found evidence the organizer has been there." She takes a large bite of her cheeseburger.

So the IBOL brochure I left for Alan has found its way into management hands. And Colby is taking her out there on one of his union-busting consulting trips. This is amusing.

"Same union?" I say.

She nods, because she is chewing.

I watch the motion of her jaw and cheek. She swallows, and there is a delicate movement in her throat.

"At least you get to go for a drive," I say.

She smiles, and I can see she is too devoted to her work to enjoy a day away from it.

Now it is her turn to watch me eat. Unused to an audience, I try to do it carefully and neatly.

We chew for a moment in silence. Then I swallow and take a sip of my soft drink. "Tell me more about what it means to stand up for yourself by sitting down," I say.

She seems gratified to have to piqued my curiosity with her remarks yesterday. She does not think about it, but starts right in. "Employers think that bringing a union into a company means mobilizing complainers," she says, "but it's not like that at all. To organize a union, you have to find people who stand up for themselves, and you rarely find such people among complainers. Complaining is what you do while you are waiting for management to solve your problems.

"Organizing is what you do to solve your own problems."

Kathleen doubtless has had some experience with organizing.

"You know everyone at the FOW," I say. "If you had

to pick the employee most likely to stand up for herself, who would it be?"

"Are you thinking about organizing us?" she says.

"It's just a game," I say. "Who would you pick?"

She thinks for a moment. "Maybe Crazy Bryce," she says at last.

I have seen Bryce around. "Why Bryce?"

"He's not at all crazy, you know."

"Why do they call him Crazy Bryce?"

"He has a strange hobby," she says. "It scares people, but it's really just a hobby."

It does not surprise me that Kathleen seems well-acquainted with a coworker who scares people. She is the kind of person people naturally open up to, which is why I have to stay on my guard with her. "What hobby?" I say.

"He studies serial killers," she says. "He knows all about them. He even has pictures of them stuck up around his work station. Jeffrey Dahmer, Ted Bundy, Vlad the Impaler."

"Vlad the Impaler?"

"You know, the guy who inspired the Dracula story."

"Do you think he's dangerous?"

"I wouldn't want to meet him in a dark place," she says.

"I thought you said it's just a hobby."

"Oh, you mean Bryce," she says. "I thought you were talking about Vlad the Impaler. Now there's a dangerous guy."

"What about Bryce? Is he dangerous?"

"No more than you are," she says. "In fact, he's a lot like you. Self-reliant. Works hard. Keeps to himself."

"But he studies serial killers," I say.

"And you play what-if games," she says.

I smile. "You would be good at this."

It pleases her, and for a moment I think she may start to preen, but she just continues to smile and bows her head to sip more root beer, drinking to the soft grating sound that signals there is nothing left in the cup but ice cubes. She puts the cup aside.

I set my plastic tray with its sandwich wrappers aside on the next table.

"May I ask you something?" she says.

"Ask."

"Where are you from?"

Perhaps I should have expected this question, but I am unprepared. I try to think what kind of story is most likely to ingratiate me.

"Is it a difficult question, Gregg?"

"I'm from Xieng Khouang," I say, "in Laos."

"I thought you were Korean," she says. It is a common mistake.

"I'm Hmong," I say.

"Why did you hesitate before telling me?"

"It's been a long time. We left there when I was nine."

"Your family?"

I clench my jaw for a moment and hesitate. "Not all of us."

She waits quietly for me to continue, and I sense I have made a connection. She knows there is a deep story here. She wants to hear it, no matter how painful it might be. I look down at the table as if overwhelmed by my memories of Laos. Then I look up to share my story with her.

"The United States stopped bombing our country in 1973. We felt safe then. Life started to return to normal. In the schoolyard one day, my friends and my brother and I were kicking around a little metal ball we found. I had to leave them to go to my afternoon job cleaning the toilets of Vietnamese immigrants. So I wasn't there when it happened."

She waits quietly for me to continue.

"The little ball turned out to be an unexploded cluster bomb. Both of my friends were injured. My brother was killed."

I let her absorb the climax of the story, which is one I read in a magazine.

When I am finished, she is staring at me seriously. "I'm sorry," she says.

"It was a long time ago."

I can tell she feels my pain. "I'm sorry," she says again.

"It does me good to talk with you about it."

She wants to know everything about the experience of being a young Hmong. I must carefully fabricate enough Asian communist lore to be convincing: the re-education of neighbors, the ruins left by more than two million tons of bombs, the muddy streets of the cities, ox-carts, Buddhist temples, hibiscus.

"That's massive," she says.

"It seemed like it at the time," I say.

"What do they do on a date?"

I realize I know nothing of Hmong sexual customs except that promiscuity is not one of them. Otherwise, I am at something of a loss.

She takes my bewilderment for discomposure. "I'm sorry. I didn't mean to disquiet you."

"It's not your fault," I say manfully. "I'm just ... " I pause for a long time. "I've never dated before," I say at last.

Interest flares in her eyes. "You've never…?"

I am her wounded animal. A creature she can care for when no one else will.

"No," I say. "I've never…" My voice trails off, my Hmong persona choked with the tragedy of my loneliness. Finally I manage to speak again. "We're very modest people," I say.

"You mean you're shy?" she says gently.

I nod. "And inexperienced. I wouldn't know how to even approach someone for…" My voice trails off again because my Hmong persona doesn't know the words that can describe his suffering or the cure for it.

She reaches across the little table and touches my hand.

Eight

When Dennis had told Colby in a telephone meeting about the call from Jolly Jim's Refresh & Refuel, Colby had seen an opportunity to make some progress in developing his own little organization and at the same time to learn something about his adversary. "IBOL," he said. "It sounds like the same guy. I'm going out there."

"Do you think it's a good idea to leave the FOW now?" said Dennis.

"It'll be OK for a day," said Colby.

"Your attention will be divided," said Dennis.

"I'm not going to be able to do anything here until I get my own organization in line," said Colby. "I'm going to use this day trip to build Kathleen's loyalty."

"She's your assistant?"

"Associate," corrected Colby. "She's a vice president of the union, for goodness' sake. Before this is over, I am going to need her to watch my back. She's bound to have misgivings about what we're doing. If I can get her off-site for a day and make her active in a prevention effort, it will go a long way toward getting her on my side."

"What does your intuition tell you?" said Dennis. "That's what I want to know."

"It's not like you to ask about my intuition," said Colby. "You're the one who's always asking for plans and evidence.

"Lathrop brought you into this case because of your intuition," said Dennis. "He didn't hire you because you're a hard worker or because you dress well. He brought you in because you have a particular talent, and he needs that talent."

Dennis was right, of course. Human beings with talent don't choose their work. It chooses them. And once chosen, the talented are driven like the wicked before the furies. Beethoven continued to write piano sonatas when he could not hear them except by holding a rod in his teeth against the instrument. Marian Evans wrote timeless, monumental novels when she had no hope of publishing except by abandoning her very identity and adopting the name George Eliot. Debbie Fields continued to bake when they told her nobody could ever franchise chocolate chip cookies.

Colby knew what it was to be tortured by an idle talent.

"Go with your gut," said Dennis.

Colby started to hang up, but Dennis stopped him.

"We got another fax from your organizer," he said.

Colby noticed it was *his* organizer now. "And?"

"It says, 'Thread the rude eye of rebellion.' Does that mean anything to you?"

"*King John*," said Colby. "It's a play by Shakespeare. One of the lesser known tragedies. Only Shakespeare said, '*Un*thread the rude eye of rebellion.' "

"King John? The one who signed the Magna Carta?"

"The English consider him the worst king they ever had," said Colby. "They don't even like his name. There has never been a John the Second."

"What do you suppose he's trying to tell us?" said Dennis.

"In the play," said Colby, "King John's offense was that he disrupted the natural order of the world."

"Natural order?" said Dennis. "Everything about this guy is an exercise in obscurity."

Colby thanked him, hung up, and tried to remember everything else he knew about King John outside of the play. It wasn't much. Wasn't Robin Hood involved somehow?

Colby punched in the number for his house. He looked at his watch while waiting for the call to connect. It was nine p.m. Frannie was always in bed reading by nine. She would probably get it on the first ring, since the telephone was on the night stand by the bed.

But she didn't get it on the first ring. It rang four times before the machine picked it up and answered in his own voice. "We're not here right now. Please leave your message after the tone."

"Frannie?"

But she didn't pick up. He knew she was there. She just wasn't going to talk to him. There wasn't any way he could get her to pick up. He'd already used up the "this is important" line. He set the phone back in its cradle and closed the compartment again.

* * *

Dennis had given him the name and number of one Irene Gettings, the single shareholder of the subchapter-S corporation that owned Jolly Jim's Refresh & Refuel. After he had worked his way, via telephone, through a lawyer, a financial advisor, and a secretary, Irene Gettings was grate-

ful to hear from him and agreed to meet him at Jolly Jim's
to discuss her union problem.

Kathleen met him in the morning at the FOW building.
He pulled the car up in front of her. He hit the switch, and
the pneumatic door sighed as it lifted itself open.

She looked a little surprised to see the door open by
itself, and Colby thought perhaps she had never ridden in a
luxury sports sedan before. She climbed in without greeting
him. Colby was pleased. He judged she was having trouble
dealing with the contradiction of her assignment. He could
not have timed this better if he'd tried.

She wore another of her brightly colored denim overalls. This pair had horizontal stripes of primary colors. She
wore a black tee shirt, which was just visible under a faded
silk jacket advertising Macon Bacon, which Colby assumed
was a special type of pork. Her earrings appeared to be
plastic spools, with the bright red sewing thread still on
them. She did not look like the vice president of operations
for a national labor union. Colby was interested to discover
that she didn't just dress that way around the office, but
went everywhere looking like the assistant to a birthday-
party clown. He wondered what that made him.

"How do you like the car?" he said.

"Magnetic."

He started to tell her that it was powered by internal
combustion, but he checked himself when he saw the way
she rubbed the leather of the upholstery. "Magnetic" was,
apparently, another of her strange affirmations. He set the
handling for PRIMARY THROUGH ROUTE, and they pulled
out of the parking lot to get to the interstate.

Once they got on the highway, he looked over at her.
They had about an hour's drive ahead. Now was a good
time to get started on her conversion.

"Have you been in the FOW long?"

"Six years." Her tone was not hostile, but she refused to look at him. "But I've only been at headquarters for a year."

"Why did you come to headquarters?"

She shrugged. "Harv thought I would do good work here. He asked me to stand for election to vice president."

"You're a politician, then," said Colby.

"Not really. I ran unopposed. Most FOW members don't want to be officers. They just want to do their jobs."

Colby decided he had enough groundwork to approach the main question. "Does it bother you to be working with me?"

Kathleen watched the scenery out her window for a moment, then spoke to the glass. "Yes."

"I thought it might," said Colby. "You're far too sensitive a person not to feel the conflicts."

"I don't know what choice I have," she said. "Harv's my boss. But I don't like this. Working to stop a union. It's adversative to my life experience."

"But you work for the members of the FOW," said Colby.

"So what?"

"The members of the FOW rely on you to protect their interests," he said. "They want their union to provide the services it is supposed to provide, not get mired in contract negotiations, formal work procedures, and excessive pay scales."

Colby had no idea what services the FOW provided its members, and he didn't really care. The important thing was to make Kathleen feel good about this.

Kathleen looked at him. "It makes sense in a twisted kind of way."

"Not a twisted kind of way," said Colby. "It makes sense in a direct way. Whoever pays your salary, whoever elected you, that's whom you work for, whether it's shareholders or union members. It's the simplest principle in the world."

"Words to live by," she said.

Colby wasn't going to let her make a joke of it. "I do live by it," he said. "So do you. You just need to admit it to yourself."

She seemed to relax, and she actually looked at him. Her expression was not unfriendly. It was as if she wanted to be his ally but just needed a rationale for it. If he could now get her to talk about herself, it would raise her receptivity.

"What does a vice president of operations at the FOW do?" he said.

"I run monitoring programs," she said, "and I go through the mail."

Not much business was done by regular mail anymore, but with nearly a hundred employees, it still sounded like an enormous job. "You open all the mail for the whole company?"

"Yeah," said Kathleen. "I open it, and I read it."

Colby was surprised she did a clerical job with such aplomb.

"I deconstruct each piece of mail."

Colby understood by this that she analyzed the mail. "How does that work?"

It was obviously a job Kathleen had mastered, for she became more animated in her explanation. "I have to record who it's from, who it's to, what it's about."

"You write a précis?"

"Oh, no. That would take too long. My software has

auto-complete. I can do a one-page letter in about forty seconds."

"What is it you do with a piece of mail? What do you give the software?"

"After I enter the from and to, there are six boxes. I put a score from zero to five in each one. Each box is a different parameter. There's one for type of service, then request, member category, issue, opinion, and personal."

Colby thought about it. Six categories to cover the breadth of human experience in the workplace. It sounded about right. He admired the elegance of the idea. After all, work (and therefore communication about work) consists of a limited repertoire of actions: we gather information, we spread information, we move things from one category to another, we decide yes or no, we postpone deciding yes or no. In any job, those actions might constitute only twenty percent of the tasks, but they take up eighty percent of the time and effort. A typical Pareto distribution.

"What happens to the data?" he said.

"Based on the scores I give it in each category, the answering system generates a reply to the letter, and then it stores the values in the addressee's profile. We build profiles of the employees based on the mail they get."

"The stuff I have to spend the most time on is personal information," said Kathleen. "Whenever I come across personal information, that's where I do have to write a précis. But there isn't very much of that in the mail these days. Most of it's in telephone conversations and e-mail, and we have software to analyze that."

No wonder Kathleen was so influential among the employees. Colby also realized the source of Lathrop's intimate knowledge of his employees' lives.

Colby realized that Kathleen could be useful in intelligence gathering. "Have you ever seen anything in the mail that looks like organizing activity?"

"No. And I think I would recognize it. I've done my share of organizing."

* * *

There was a black limousine parked in front of the restaurant at Jolly Jim's Refresh & Refuel. The passenger compartment windows were mirrored, so it was not possible to see if there was anyone inside, but a chauffeur was sitting at the steering wheel, reading a magazine, which he probably would not have done if his passengers were on board.

Colby parked the car, and he and Kathleen entered the restaurant, which was the largest presence at the truck stop, and went looking for an office. At the back of the building, removed from the public areas of the restaurant, they found a door marked "Private."

He knocked.

After a moment the door opened partway and a pleasant-looking woman looked out. She was middle-aged and slightly overweight. Her face wore a harried expression. She pointed down the hall.

"The rest rooms are that way."

"I'm Stillman Colby."

She apparently recognized the name, but she did not lose her harried expression when she opened the door wider. "Come in."

She walked back into the office.

Colby and Kathleen followed her. The office was cramped, but there was already someone else in it. A fashion model. She may have been the most nearly perfect woman Colby had ever seen. It took only a moment, however, for him to understand that she was not perfect. She was better than perfect, for if she were indeed a fashion model, she was about ninety days past her prime and had begun to acquire a hint of a most desirable fleshiness at her hips and chest. Her lips were full and her honey-colored hair was pulled into a knot at the back, echoing the austerity of a gray suit.

"This is Irene Gettings." The woman who had let them in gestured to the fashion model. "I'm Melissa Willard, the manager here."

Colby shook Irene Gettings' hand. He admired the technique of her handshake (a firm grip without any squeezing, a single shake, then relax and withdraw), but it was too perfect a gesture to make any kind of human connection.

"This is my associate, Kathleen," said Colby.

Irene Gettings took Kathleen's hand. She was apparently too polite to let her surprise register on her face, but Colby's intuition told him she disapproved of Kathleen's clothing.

Irene Gettings turned back to face him. "You'll solve my problem for me?"

"One way or another." Colby smiled and reached toward the other woman.

Melissa Willard had apparently never had any training in handshakes, for she grasped Colby's hand with as much enthusiasm as if she were standing in quicksand.

Her hand was tense, and the dampness in her palm spoke volumes to Colby about the woman's relationship to her boss and the security of her position.

"I understand you found a pamphlet," he said.

"Yes," she said, "out on one of the fuel islands."

Colby looked at Irene Gettings. He needed to get these people to relax. "By itself, a pamphlet doesn't always mean anything." He turned back to Melissa Willard and watched as an invisible hand removed a coat hanger from the back of her shirt.

"I don't need a union here," said Irene Gettings, as if she believed Colby were a visitor from another planet, in need of a basic business education.

"Let's find out from Melissa if you've got one," he said.

They all sat to listen to Melissa Willard's story. The pamphlet she had found was from IBOL. She passed it around. Irene Gettings gasped audibly when it was put into her hands, and she shook her head emphatically as she turned its pages.

The pamphlet offered the usual claptrap about personal dignity, fairness, and justice. It said that in the old days, as much as a third of the country's workers belonged to unions. Colby thought the current proportion was around one quarter. The pamphlet also said it was well known that the most profitable companies were union shops.

There was a way in which Colby envied the people who wrote union pamphlets. The things they wrote did not have to be true. Who is going to challenge it?

"It's nothing special," he said. "All unions publish these little pamphlets. This doesn't even mean they have approached your people. An organizer could have left this where you would find it, just to make you feel threatened. If he scares you, that's half of what he's after."

"What kind of sick person gets satisfaction from something like that?" said Irene Gettings.

"Nobody knows what drives a person into labor organizing," said Colby.

"Is there no protection from such creatures?" said Irene Gettings.

From the corner of his eye, Colby could see Kathleen

shifting uncomfortably in her chair. If she got through this meeting without braining Irene Gettings, she would be well along to where Colby wanted her.

"The pamphlet by itself means nothing," said Colby again. "Your company may be a target, and it may not." This was one of his best phrases for making a sale of prevention services. Business owners focused so predictably on the *may be a target* part, that they never seemed to hear the *may not* part.

"My father would die if the unions got in here," said Irene Gettings.

Colby thought this a rather strange remark, since he had understood from Dennis that Ms. Gettings's father was already dead. He turned to Melissa Willard.

"Can you show me the scene?"

* * *

After he'd had the chance to study the area where the pamphlet was found, he asked Melissa Willard if he could interview the people who had been on the shift when she found it. Irene Gettings wanted to be there, and Colby suggested she act only as an observer. She agreed.

He told Kathleen to take Melissa somewhere private and get more details from her about the truck stop's staff and routines. This would be a good opportunity to show her that managers are human beings, too. If she got to know Melissa Willard, she might appreciate how the organizer had put the woman's job at risk.

The absence of the other two women seemed to relax Irene Gettings, who was apparently uncomfortable around Kathleen.

"I take it this is the young woman's day job," she said.

Colby looked at her beautiful, smug face. "She's the most capable associate I've ever had," he said.

The shift crew consisted of four men and two women. The first one, the shift supervisor, set the tone for all the interviews.

"What pamphlet?" he said.

Colby questioned them all and was pleased to learn that none of them knew anything about the pamphlet. None of them even reacted to the suggestion a labor organizer might have been around – none except a young man named Alan.

"What does he look like?" said Alan.

"We don't know," said Colby. "That's one of the things we'd like to learn from you. Has anyone talked to you about labor unions?"

"No," said Alan.

Colby thanked him for his time and let him leave. After the boy had gone back to the fuel island, Colby turned to Irene Gettings. "He knows something."

It did not seem to concern the woman how Colby understood this. "I'll have Melissa fire him."

"He's an at-will employee, and you're within your rights," said Colby. "But we'll have a better chance to track down the organizer if we leave him on the job and watch him."

"Do you know what you're asking?"

Before Colby could answer, there was a deedling sound from her handbag. She opened it and pulled out a small telephone.

"Yes?"

Colby knew what he was asking. He was asking this woman to remain open to the possibility of a labor union just so he had a chance of finding the organizer. It was a great deal to ask of any employer.

"How is the mother doing? Five, you say?"

How to keep the employee at work and thus under surveillance while protecting Irene Gettings from the effects of unionization? Fortunately, Colby had experience in fashioning creative solutions to just this kind of dilemma.

"Make sure she's comfortable and that the doctor checks her before he leaves." She folded the phone closed and returned it to her handbag. She was smiling. "Five kittens. All healthy. The mother's doing fine." Then her smile vanished as she returned to the business at hand. "I can't spend much more time on this. Let's get Melissa in here and take care of that boy." She turned toward the door as if she might summon the manager by force of will.

"I have a suggestion to make, Ms. Gettings," said Colby.

She turned back toward him and waited.

"You can fire them all, but leave them in place on the job."

"Are you crazy, Mr. Colby?"

"Ms. Gettings, have you ever heard of employee leasing?"

* * *

It took one phone call to Dennis to put the Jolly Jim's Refresh & Refuel organizing problem into the hands of Preventive Leasing, Inc. Irene Gettings could return to her cats knowing her company was even less of a problem to her than when Melissa first found the pamphlet.

Colby gave Melissa a checklist of signs to watch for in

dealing with Alan until the Protective Leasing, Inc. monitors arrived. He asked her to note if she saw any outsiders talking to the young man and to call him if she did.

It was a routine job, but Colby judged it had its desired effect. After getting a pep talk this morning and spending the afternoon with a fairly desperate manager, Kathleen seemed much more at ease with her current assignment. On the drive back to the FOW headquarters, she was voluble. "I didn't know this work would be suscitating," she said. "An idea and a phone call, and it changes a whole operation." She snapped her thumb, which wore an ornate ring, against her finger. "Like that."

Colby recognized the signs of someone who likes power. Kathleen was a charming person, and she was also a power groupie.

"Where are you from?" She twisted the ring on her thumb.

"North of here," he said.

"How long have you been a prevention consultant?"

Colby did not want to tell her anything about his personal life. He shrugged.

"Let me tell you a story," he said.

"What for?"

"I think stories are a good way to communicate," said Colby.

"Why don't you just tell me what you want to tell me?"

"This will be more meaningful." Colby wondered why she was being so thick.

"OK," she said. "Tell me a story."

"This is a story about a young man with an MBA and a desire to do some good in the world."

"An ASS?"

"He didn't think about such things in those days," said Colby, "but I suppose you could call him an ASS-in-training."

"Let me guess," she said. "He went to work for a labor relations consulting firm."

"Not right away," said Colby. "His first job was with a Big Five services firm. He did management capability assessments for the consulting division. It was a fast-track job, and everyone knew the MBA would be a division head within five years."

"Did he like the work?"

"He loved it," said Colby. "He wanted to do it forever."

"What happened?"

"Family emergency," said Colby. "The MBA had a younger brother, and the brother got mixed up with a bad crowd."

"At school?"

"No. He was out of school. He was working for a large insurance company in a dead-end job pushing numbers. Unfortunately for him, the company attracted the notice of a union – the Fraternity of Accounting and Support Staff. They infiltrated the company, and one of their operatives approached the brother. The boy was going through a bad patch just then."

"What do you mean by 'bad patch'?"

"He had just broken up with his girlfriend. And his older brother was a smashing success while he felt he was in a dead-end job. The kind of problems that many young people have at one time or another. But this union preyed on things like that. The man who approached him knew just what buttons to push. Pretty soon, he had a signed membership card from him."

Kathleen nodded. She knew the significance of signing a membership card.

"They put him up in a new apartment, and he thought that was just great. He didn't realize it was another of their control methods. It allowed them to watch him after hours as well as at work. They gradually assumed control of almost every aspect of his life."

"But if he had a new apartment—"

"It was a golden cage. And at work they made him recruit others with the union's message of working for a 'higher purpose' in business and the promise of a 'better life to come.' What did any of these kids know? They were all young, separated from their families in dead-end jobs. They were very vulnerable. They all lived together in the brother's fancy apartment. They spent the evenings chanting, meditating, and singing.

"But productivity in the brother's section began to decline because all these young people were thinking about other things and weren't concentrating on their jobs. Management took notice and decided to bring in consultants to find out what was going on. As luck would have it, they brought in the MBA brother's firm."

"What a coincidence," said Kathleen.

"Not really," said Colby. "His firm had one of the best consulting services in the business, and this insurance company was one of the richest insurance companies. They tended to hire the best. The MBA brother was the head of the consulting team. He liked working in his brother's department. It was great to have the opportunity to see him and eat lunch with him from time to time.

"But the MBA brother was so intent on his work that he didn't even notice how deeply troubled his brother was. He found evidence of union organizing, but he didn't put two and two together, and had no idea his brother was involved. The day before he submitted his report to the insurance company's management detailing his findings about the union, he mentioned it to his younger brother at lunch. It was just a passing comment. Maybe he even said it to show how important he was. He certainly didn't think he was tipping off the union.

"The next day, all those young people living at the brother's apartment poisoned themselves. They were found lying in their beds with notes pinned to their neckties. The notes all said the same thing: 'We strive together for a better world.' "

"That's dolorous," said Kathleen. "I'm so sorry."

Colby said nothing. He was surprised at the depth of emotion he had roused in himself with this impromptu account. It was almost as if it were true.

They were silent for a moment, then Kathleen spoke again.

"Thank you for opening up to me like that."

Colby shrugged as if it were nothing.

"Why do they call you Cole?" she said.

"It's just a nickname," said Colby absently.

"Why not Still? Why don't they call you Still?"

"Some people do," said Colby.

"Do you mind if I call you Still?"

Disorientation welled up in him. Frannie called him Still. He was driving up the highway at twilight with a young woman he barely knew, and she was asking if she might address him like family.

His intuition said if he told her not to use the name, she would sense some weakness and use it anyway.

"OK," he said softly.

"Good," she said. "From now on, you're Still."

He looked at her, and she was smiling. The gold light of the sunset washed over her skin and brightened her outlandish jewelry, if that were possible. Why would anyone dangle thread spools from her ear lobes? And yet, she was pretty in her multicolored overalls. Colby remembered the first time he'd seen her and how he thought she looked like hard candy. She didn't look like hard candy now. Hard was not a word that could be applied to her in any sense. Colby found himself imagining what it would be like to kiss her – to feel her fleshy lips with his, to explore her perfectly aligned teeth with his tongue. He pushed the thought out of his mind. She was young enough to be his daughter.

"Where are you from, Kathleen?"

"Xieng Khouang," she said. "I'm from Laos."

"You don't look Asian," said Colby.

"Ethnically I'm not," she said. "My parents were missionaries."

"What was it like growing up there?" said Colby.

Kathleen shrugged. "What's it like anywhere? Charming villages, hibiscus, cities with muddy streets, government run by communist satraps."

Colby was fascinated. He wondered if growing up in Laos had informed her taste in clothing.

"I lost a childhood friend to unexploded ordinance," she said.

"I'm sorry," said Colby.

"We had been kicking a little metal ball around the schoolyard," she said. "I had to leave early, because my parents were strict about making me get home soon after school was out. I was lucky, I guess."

They were quiet for a time, until Kathleen broke the silence again.

"It was wonderful what you did for Melissa, Still," said Kathleen. "She was really afraid of her boss. I'm glad you saved her job for her."

"I didn't do it for her," said Colby. "It just happened that doing my job saved hers."

"I don't think you're giving yourself enough credit, bwana," she said. "You're a humanitarian."

Colby wondered if he could trust that Kathleen meant the same thing by the word "humanitarian" that he did. She often seemed to talk like someone who had memorized an obsolete thesaurus. And why did she call him *bwana*? Was that a Laotian term?

He looked at her, and she was smiling at him. She wasn't trying to ridicule him. She admired what he had done out there at Jolly Jim's. He wasn't used to admiration from women. He and Frannie had an excellent relationship, but he would be hard put to claim she admired him. Most of what he considered to be his accomplishments, she considered antics. His most idealistic impulses were to her childish.

The outlandish earrings dangled from Kathleen's ear lobes. One of them hung lower than the other. It appeared to be loose. He wondered if he should say something to her about it. Was it too personal to point out to a woman that she had a loose earring? Or a loose spool, as the case may be?

He looked back at the road. Better not to notice.

Back at the FOW, as he nosed the sports sedan into the parking lot, he encountered a short convoy of two minivans leaving. Each bore a logo: *C&B: Union Carpenters.*

"Are we remodeling?" said Colby.

"Could be," said Kathleen.

He pulled into a parking space, shifted the car into park, and turned off the ignition. He turned to Kathleen.

She was quite pretty. She could be an attractive woman if she'd learn how to dress.

"I guess I'll see you in the morning." She made no effort to get out of the car.

"Tomorrow," he said, "I want you to help me draw up a list of the most influential employees. Those are the ones we will work on. And I have to start individual sessions with the supervisors as well." He turned and stared at the building, more to keep himself from looking at her than to see anything there.

"Sure," she said.

She seemed to be pretty well adjusted to her conflicts. Colby counted this a day well spent. He turned to say good-bye, and found her leaning toward him in the darkness.

Colby responded by taking her in his arms. He started to kiss her.

She turned her head aside, and his kiss landed on her jaw.

"There it is," she said. She slipped out of his arms and bent down to the floor.

Colby, his arms empty, had a bad feeling, like he'd made a mistake.

Kathleen straightened up. There was a thread spool in her hand. "Almost lost an earring."

Colby realized she'd not been leaning toward him but bending over to retrieve her spool. He recoiled. "I'm sorry."

She looked at him quizzically, as if wondering what he was talking about.

But he was too embarrassed to say anything else.

"It's late. I have to egress." She opened the door and climbed out.

Colby did not look at her. He stared at the floor of the car and concentrated his energies on disappearing. It didn't work.

"Good night." She closed the door.

Colby sat in silence for a moment, wondering if he could possibly feel stupider.

He finally looked up. Kathleen was long gone. What kind of compartment had he opened this time?

Nine

I hold the first meeting of my organizing committee in my room at the Select Suites Hotel. I call room service and order a dinner for two of fruit and sandwiches.

I ask the room service waiter to set up the tray on the table in my room. He arranges the places while I sign the check. When he leaves, he encounters my organizing committee on its way in.

Crazy Bryce, the self-reliant student of serial killers, treads warily into the room.

Crazy Bryce is intrigued by the secrecy under which I invited him here and the danger it implies. At my invitation, we sit and I offer him sandwiches. He isn't in a position to turn down free food, but he eats guardedly.

We do not chat, but methodically devour everything. We finish and push the plates aside. I judge the food has relaxed him a little.

"Employers think that bringing a union into a company means mobilizing complainers," I say, "but it's not like that at all. To organize a union, you have to find people who stand up for themselves, and you rarely find such people among complainers. Complaining is what you do while you are waiting for management to solve your problems.

"Organizing is what you do to solve your own problems."

When Kathleen said it, it had seemed persuasive, but it doesn't have very much effect on Bryce.

"Why did you pick me out?" he says.

His tone is suspicious, and I realize I need to establish some level of trust. He opened up to Kathleen. I decide to use her name.

"Kathleen recommended you," I say. "She says you are someone who will stand up for yourself."

"Kathleen?" he says. "Is she in on this?"

"She's a supporter," I say. "But the first rule is that you never expose a supporter, so you can't tell anyone. You shouldn't even mention it to her, even if you think you're alone with her. I have thoroughly checked this room, and it is the only safe place to discuss organizing activities. Everywhere else, they are watching and listening."

"Who?"

"The union," I say. "You may work for a union, but unless you're an executive, they don't want you to belong to one. They don't want you to have representation in your dealings with management."

"Why should I want to join yours?" he says.

"I won't lie to you," I say. "We can't promise you a pay increase or job security. In fact, you could lose your job."

"Then what's the point?" he says.

"The point is a chance to stand up for yourself," I say.

I give it a moment to sink in, and I can see it is working. When I judge that the idea has softened him up, I push deeper. "Management doesn't want you to stand up for yourself. Management puts no value on that particular effort. In fact, management considers it a cost. They'd rather not have you around if you have a backbone. But IBOL wants people who stand up for themselves. We value that in people."

Kathleen's assessment of him was accurate. He does like the idea of standing up for himself, and he is flattered to have someone recognize it, even someone he barely knows and has every reason to distrust. I find myself pleased to be working with him rather than with my first prospect. He is harder to win over, but he will be easier to trust. And apparently, I won't have to date him.

"Many people will hate you if they think you are doing organizing work," I say. "But people often hate their protectors."

He is a loner, and I can see that the idea of being despised by the people he protects has some appeal for him.

"Most people don't have the stomach for this work," I say. "They don't like stalking, they don't like having a secret life. They don't like the idea that they may be called on to be utterly ruthless."

He is even more alert now, and I can see he follows my every word.

"To be a union organizer," I say, "you have to lead a double life. You have to seem perfectly normal to the people you work with, but on the inside you are constantly on your guard – and plotting your next move. In some ways, it's like being a serial killer."

* * *

I go to call on Kathleen, who greets me at the door of her apartment. Her head is wrapped in a towel.

She is friendly but not as enthusiastic as she was the evening before. She invites me in and offers me a soft drink. We sit on her sofa and sip our soft drinks.

"What can I do for you?" she says.

I have forgotten why it is I have come.

"The soft drink's enough," I say, aware that I must finish it and leave. "How did things go at the truck stop today?"

"Cogent," she says. She unwraps the towel from her head. Her hair is wet – and blond.

"Cogent." It seems a positive sort of word, so I assume she is telling me it went well.

"Still set up an employee leasing program." She begins to rub her hair with the towel.

"Still?"

"It's short for Stillman," she says. "That's his first name."

I recognize the nickname, and I realize with a start that Kathleen is infatuated with Colby.

"What's employee leasing?" I say, even though I know it very well. It is one of management's more exotic tools for sidestepping its responsibility to its employees.

"Irene Gettings – she's the owner of the truck stop – lets all her employees go. They get hired by a leasing company, and she rents them back."

"What's the point of that?"

"She doesn't have to worry about managing them anymore. The leasing company takes care of that. Still convinced her to do it to keep her from firing a worker that he wants to keep an eye on."

Alan will be more receptive when I tell him how close he came to losing his job.

"Sounds clever," I say.

"Still is very conversant."

Kathleen, who has been a union activist, is so enchanted by this man and his methods that she doesn't even see she is now thinking like management.

"What's next for the FOW?" I say.

"Still wants me to find the company's most influential employees so he can counsel them."

I know this strategy. He will "counsel" them with cash payments and promises.

"You'll be good at that," I say.

"I'm going to start with Lauren," she says.

Lauren works in facilities. She is not a manager, but she runs the department. She controls nearly everything at the site. From changing a lightbulb to installing a phone line, nothing happens without her involvement. She's a good choice.

I have what I need now, but I cannot get my mind off what I want. I realize I want Kathleen. It is a futile desire. She may be interested in the exotic Hmong security guard, but not for a relationship. For that, I fear, she would look to her new interest.

Ten

Colby ate no breakfast. He did not count the number of times he had gone over the incident in his mind, but he was certain it was approaching one thousand. Did he really think Kathleen wanted him to kiss her? She was half his age. And she was his assistant, for goodness' sake. Was this sexual assault on a subordinate? He had never done such a thing before.

The questions and reproaches roiled his mind as he made his way to the elevator. He nearly tripped over a room service tray on the floor in the hallway. It rattled when his foot caught it, and he looked down. Fruit peels and pits, sandwich crusts. Long toothpicks with frilly colored decorations.

He found the elevator and rode down five floors with his mind on Kathleen. He wondered if she would have an attorney in the office waiting for him. It was what he deserved. How could he have been so stupid?

Attorney or not, he decided, he would beg her forgiveness. He had abused her trust. He had to make her understand it was a moment of insanity brought on by loneliness of the most intense kind.

But when he opened the door, she was not there. He was reminded how truly lonely an empty office can be. He walked deliberately past her desk to his own office and sat heavily in the chair. Had she decided to stop working for him? This was bad.

Colby sat at his desk for nearly an hour, torturing himself with silent reproaches and trying to think of ways to take back what he had done. It was futile, of course.

Then, about an hour after starting time, he heard stirring in the outer office. He got up and went to look, and his heart sank when he saw a woman in a beige business suit with her back to him, bending over the desk and putting something in the drawer. Lathrop had sent him a temp.

The woman closed the drawer and stood up. She turned around, and it was Kathleen. Colby was astounded at her appearance. What happened to the colorful overalls and high-top sneakers? She was even wearing ordinary earrings – small gold studs. Her hair was neatly arranged – and blond.

"Good morning, Still," she said. "Sorry I'm late. I had to pick up some things." She held up a report of some sort. "Employee list."

You look nice. The words sounded in Colby's mind, but he didn't dare say them. He was afraid to say anything.

"Shouldn't we get started?" Kathleen sat down at her desk, ran her finger along the list of employee names, and began to dial the telephone.

Colby walked around in front of her desk. "Wait."

She turned and looked up at him.

"I have to talk with you," he said.

She put the telephone receiver back in its cradle and folded her hands in front of her on the desk.

It was an unexpected pose, and Colby wondered if she was mocking him. He took a breath and forged ahead. "Kathleen, I owe you an apology and an explanation."

She waited.

Fatigue settled on him like nightfall, and he felt the loneliness of a man far from home. He could not fight it. He sat heavily in the chair, then reached up and pinched the bridge of his nose.

"Is something wrong, Still?"

Colby's throat burned and his voice was hoarse when he answered her. "My wife didn't want me to come on this assignment. Now she won't answer my telephone calls." He stared at the carpeting. He heard Kathleen rise from her chair, followed by footfalls. When he looked up, she was standing next to his chair.

She put her hand on his shoulder.

"I'm sorry," said Colby.

"What for?" she said.

"Last night," he said. "I behaved inexcusably."

"Last night?" She paused in thought. "Oh, you mean that kiss thing?"

Colby nodded without speaking.

Kathleen laughed lightly. "I accept your apology."

Colby's ears burned. He did not like being laughed at. "Is this funny?"

She took her hand from his shoulder. "As funny as a dancing bear," she said.

Colby wasn't sure if he should feel relieved or offended.

"It's not in a bear's nature to dance," she said. "When you see one do it, it's funny."

* * *

Colby gave Kathleen a wide berth for the rest of the morning. He paced his office, pausing at the doorway from time to time to watch her make her telephone calls. He took care not to stare at her too long, because he didn't want her to turn around and see him. It's difficult to face a person who thinks you're a dancing bear.

The first supervisor to arrive for a private session with Colby was a middle-aged man with mottled skin who wore his hair at shoulder length. He looked a little ill at ease in a suit. He sat across from Colby and watched him like he would watch a poisonous snake. He kept both feet flat on the floor, apparently prepared to rise suddenly if things got difficult.

Colby looked at the card Kathleen had prepared for him. It said his name was Frank and that he ran the production department.

"You run the production department, right, Frank?" Colby leaned back in his chair to create a more relaxed mood.

"Yes," said Frank. "We do editing, design, and layout for the union's brochures and newsletters."

"Proofreading?"

Frank nodded. He apparently judged he was reasonably safe, for he took his gaze off Colby and trained it on the carpet in front of his desk.

Colby decided to get right down to business. "Do you know how many of your people have signed membership cards for IBOL, Frank?"

"I don't know. Until the other day, I never even heard of IBOL."

Colby's intuition told him that Frank might not be completely on board with the prevention campaign. "It might not be easy to keep tabs on people, Frank, but it's something we're all going to have to do. Do you remember at the meeting the other day when I said we were in the fight of our lives? I wasn't joking. If we don't stop IBOL, you and I both are likely to wind up unemployed."

The threat didn't seem to persuade Frank at all, for he continued to stare at the carpet.

"Is something bothering you, Frank?"

Colby's question hung in the air for a long moment.

Finally Frank looked up. "I'm a skilled production manager," he said. "I could work anywhere. I could work at a magazine or agency. But I chose to work here because I believe in unions."

So there it was again. More hand-holding was needed.

"Are you a member of a union, Frank?"

Frank shook his head. "That doesn't have anything to do with anything," he said. "I'm not eligible to be a member of a union because I'm supervisory staff. But unions are what we stand for here, and if our people want to join a union, who are we to stop them?"

"Do you feel any loyalty to your employer, Frank?"

"Harvey Lathrop?"

"Not Harvey Lathrop," said Colby. "He's not your employer. Your employer is the collective membership of the FOW. Those are the people you're here to work for. Do you feel any loyalty to them?"

"Sure," said Frank uneasily.

"The members of the FOW rely on you to protect their interests," said Colby. "They want their union to provide the services it is supposed to provide, not get mired in contract negotiations, formal work procedures, and excessive pay scales."

Frank stared at Colby with disgust. "There's such a thing as solidarity."

"These people pay your *salary*, Frank. They've put up a matching share of your retirement funds. They depend on you. Are you willing to make the decision for them about whether the costs of running their union should increase?"

Frank said nothing.

"You can't serve two masters, Frank," said Colby. "You can be loyal to this idea of solidarity of yours, or you can be loyal to the people who pay you and depend on you. The choice is yours."

Frank continued to say nothing, and Colby's intuition told him he'd broken through. But he knew he shouldn't push it.

"Think about this stuff, Frank," said Colby. "Let's meet again tomorrow and chat about it some more."

Eleven

One of the disadvantages of a security job is that you have time to think about things. And sitting at my desk in the reception area, I find myself thinking about Kathleen. I may have allowed myself to get emotionally involved. This has never happened to me before.

The door to the work area opens and I can hear the whine of power saws and the chock chock chock of nail guns. The sound fades when the door closes. Lauren from facilities comes past my desk on her way out.

"Lauren," I say.

She stops, then turns and walks over to my desk. She is not a vivacious person, and I judge she doesn't date much. But she isn't unfriendly.

I try to think of some sort of conversational gambit.

"How long will the carpenters be here?" I say.

"It's hard to tell," she says. "Harv has ordered a complete remodeling of the building."

"What for?"

She shrugs, but she makes no effort to leave, so I judge my effort to start a conversation has been successful.

"You're on your way to the hotel, aren't you?"

"How did you know?"

"I know how these things work," I say. "The consultant wants to bring you into the union-busting program."

"Me?"

"They need to make sure you're on their side," I say.

"Why me?"

"You control facilities. You're one of the most powerful people at headquarters."

She does not dispute this. "How do you know so much about this, Gregg?"

"Union busting is a hobby of mine."

"It's a bizarre hobby," she says.

We have begun to connect.

"Do you like Flashburger?" I say.

"Who doesn't?" she says.

"How about a cheeseburger after your meeting's over?"

"That sounds nice," she says.

"Good. It's a date, then."

She smiles. She turns to leave.

"Lauren," I say.

She turns back to face me.

"He's going to offer you a cash payment."

She looks startled at this news.

"It's part of the method," I say. "They want to buy your loyalty."

"Real money?" she says.

"You don't strike me as the kind of person who can be bought," I say. "You impress me as a person willing to stand up for herself."

"I could use some extra money," she says.

"That's why I think you should take it," I say. "Just don't let them convince you they're really buying you."

"Thanks for the advice, Gregg," she says. "I'll see you later."

* * *

When next I convene my organizing committee, it has two members instead of one.

"Does either of you have any membership cards for me?" I say.

Lauren hands me two signed cards. Bryce hands me one. Three cards. Organizing is always slow work in the beginning, but we cannot afford a slow start this time.

I check the cards to make certain my organizers have properly witnessed the signatures of their prospective members and that they have gotten addresses and telephone numbers from the signers. I open my briefcase and take out the list of employees we have compiled, so I can check off the names.

I check off the names and lay the list out on the table. "Bryce, write down the names from here to here." I mark off twenty names. "Lauren, write down these." I mark off another twenty. "You each need to bring me fifteen new cards at next week's meeting."

"That's a lot of cards," says Bryce.

"I know," I say. "But we don't have much time. Your involvement with Colby buys us a little time, but not much. We have thirty days, at the outside, to get enough membership and then petition for the election. After that, whatever support we've built up begins to erode, because our members don't see any benefit in it."

They both appear a little droopy to me. I must boost their spirits. "It's always like this in the early stages," I say.

My remark doesn't seem to help much. I decide that I can bolster their resolve with a little training. "A friend of mine, my mentor, will be here shortly," I say. "But before she gets here, I want to go over some recruiting techniques with you. Bryce, tell me how you approach a prospect."

"Well," he says, "I say something like, 'Don't you hate

the way the person at the next desk comes in late and leaves early when you're here trying to get some work done?'"

I nod vigorously.

He smiles.

"It's a good idea to open the conversation indirectly like that," I say. "But how do you know that's what is bothering the prospect?"

"It's the biggest problem at the union," he says. "No accountability."

"Yes, it is the biggest problem at the union. But does it bother everybody else as much as it bothers you?"

I can see a flicker of recognition in his eyes. "No, I guess not," he says. "Everybody seems to have a different gripe about the union."

"Exactly," I say.

He smiles, and I can see the lesson is working.

"If everybody has a different gripe with the union," I say, "why don't you go after your prospects based on their individual gripes?"

"Yeah," he says.

"How do we do that?" says Lauren.

"Try friendly conversation," I say. "You are talking with someone, and you say, 'If there was one thing you could change about this union, what would it be?' Then the person will say, 'the guy at the next desk would come in on time and stay the whole day.' Then what do you say?"

"If we were unionized," says Lauren, "there would be work rules and everybody would pull their own weight."

"Now what if the prospect says, 'we need different toppings on the Friday chalupas'?"

"What do chalupas have to do with anything?" says Bryce.

"They are crucial if they are what the prospect cares about," I say. "And if the prospect says having different chalupa toppings on Fridays is the one change that needs to be made, you say, 'If we were unionized, we could negotiate for better toppings.'"

They look dubious.

There is a knock at the door.

I get up and go over to open the door.

"Hello, Frannie."

"Hi, Gregg."

Twelve

It had been a long time since he had done this, and by the time Colby had interviewed four employees, he was exhausted. It was nearing the end of the day anyway, so he decided to knock off a little early and go back to his hotel room to study. He had a copy of *The Noncooperative Economy* by Harvey Lathrop. He wanted to use it to get some insight into his client.

He walked past Kathleen's desk. She was rummaging in the drawers. She looked up and saw him.

"I used to have a stick of lip balm," she said. "I guess I left it in my other desk." She saw the book in his hand.

"You can't be that lonely, Still," she said.

"Have you read it?"

She shook her head. "I didn't have to. I know the author."

Something in her tone told him that she knew him in a way that would be impolite to ask about.

"I'll see you tomorrow," said Colby.

Back in his room, Colby removed his jacket and necktie and hung them in the closet; then he sat down at the desk and opened the book. He skipped over the preface and the introduction and began reading a chapter called "The Grace of the Corporation."

The corporation is the primary mechanism for creating and distributing wealth in modern society. We take this for granted today, but before there were corporations, wealth was controlled and distributed by three forces: the state (usually a king), the church (in many ways, the precursor of the modern corporation), and caprice. The result was a great concentration of society's wealth in the hands of the few. This was a consumptive society, and although fortunes were built and maintained by great families and institutions, there was no capital formation. Real investment had to wait for the advent of the limited liability corporation, which began its slow development in early modern times.

Colby had no idea Lathrop was capable of seeing life in these terms. The man actually seemed to admire what the corporation had done for society. He skipped ahead until he found a subtitle for "The Modern Corporation."

Over the long term, the corporation has been able to achieve ascendancy over all other collective institutions with which it has competed. Alone among modern organizations, it enjoys the rights and freedoms of a natural person.

Associations, such as labor unions and professional associations, are restricted by their charters to activities that benefit their members. Churches are restricted to activities that serve particular religions. Governments are restricted to certain jurisdictions. A corporation, on the other hand, operates from a charter so generalized that it can change the nature and objectives of its business without amending it. As long as it operates within the law, it can change from manufacturing to service and back again without rechartering. It can change its location at will, and it is answerable only to its owners.

Colby was impressed. This man had a lucid understanding of society and the role of the corporation. What was he doing running a labor union? He glanced at his watch and realized he should try to call Frannie now, so he wouldn't interrupt her dinner. He closed the book, picked up the telephone, and dialed his house.

But once again he got no answer.

In his gut, uncertainty mixed with anxiety like a poisoned chowder as he set the telephone receiver in its cradle. He felt weak, and he remembered that he had not eaten all day. He picked up the telephone receiver again and started to dial room service. There was a knock at the door.

Colby got up and went to the door. He looked through the peep hole, and the fisheye lens revealed Kathleen smiling at the door. She held a large covered basket in one hand and a brightly colored paper bag in the other. She thrust the colored bag up toward the peep hole.

"Room service," she said.

Colby opened the door.

Kathleen held the bag out to him. "Cheeseburgers."

She had changed her beige business suit for jeans and a tee shirt.

"Kathleen," said Colby. "That's very kind of you, but maybe it's not a good idea."

"Have you already eaten?" she said.

"As a matter of fact, I haven't," he said.

She pushed past him into the room. "This looks to me like a cheeseburger emergency, Still."

Colby was helpless before the surge of her energy. She opened her basket and removed a tablecloth, which she spread over the table. Then she set out paper plates, a bottle of wine, and two glasses. Finally, she unwrapped several cheeseburgers, which appeared to come from a place called Flashburger, and set them on the plates, with french fries.

Colby followed her orders and sat down at the table to eat with her. She made no conversation but attacked her cheeseburger methodically, taking three or four french fries after every second bite of burger. He followed her lead, and he was surprised at the calming effect the food had on him.

When the cheeseburgers and fries were gone, they pushed their chairs out from the table and sipped wine for several minutes without speaking. Colby felt restored.

Finally Kathleen spoke. "Sometimes the best thing you can do for a man is get a cheeseburger in him. How do you like *The Noncooperative Economy*?"

"I've just gotten started," said Colby.

"Everybody dies at the end," she said.

Colby laughed.

"Nice room." Kathleen put down her wine glass and looked around. "And it must be wonderful to have somebody come in every day and pick up after you." She got up and walked over to the dresser. "Don't you just love bobinga?" She rubbed its surface with her hand. She bent low, then leaned over and rubbed her cheek on the dresser, a gesture that was at once innocent and sensual.

"You always expect the best from people, don't you?" he said.

She laughed. "What's that supposed to mean?"

Colby felt his ears burn. He couldn't believe he had said anything so personal.

She laughed again. "I could light a candle on one of your ears."

She sat down again. She was smiling now, and it occurred to Colby that Kathleen's eyes were her best feature. Sparkling bronze irises surrounded by flawless ivory.

It was getting late, but the thought of sitting in this

room alone chilled him and he could not bring himself to say anything about the hour.

"How do *you* manage the issues?" she said.

"What issues?"

"Yesterday you explained all about loyalty to me," she said, "But you never said anything about your own conflicts."

"What conflicts?"

"It must give you contention," she said, "working for a union against a union."

"As far as I'm concerned," said Colby, "there are no issues. I'm here to stand up for a principle."

She looked at him as if he might be a visitor from another dimension of space-time. "Principle?"

"The principle of serving my client," said Colby. "If there are issues, they are my client's issues, not mine."

The two of them sat in silence while Colby's remark hung in the air.

"Principle," repeated Kathleen, only this time it sounded more like an observation than a question.

Colby thought it might be a good idea to take the conversation in a less principled direction.

"How did you get involved with the union?" he said.

Kathleen shrugged, then stood up and started toward him.

Colby was sorry she was preparing to leave. He stood up.

She extended her hand.

Colby started to take it, but she laid it flat on his chest.

The warmth of her touch was like magic, and all thought of principles fled his mind. He grabbed her shoulders and kissed her mouth, pressing her arms and hands between them. Her lips were soft, and she kept her mouth open. His tongue sought hers and caressed it.

She freed her hands and grabbed the back of his neck. She tasted like cheeseburger, and somehow that made the kiss even more intimate.

He felt his erection strain against his clothes.

When the kiss ended, Colby pressed his face to her neck and enjoyed her soapy smell.

Without knowing how he got there, Colby found himself lying on the bedspread with his arms around her. He kissed her again, but then she worked her way out of his embrace.

Colby realized it had gone too far, and he steeled himself to say good night.

But working her way out of his embrace turned out to be part of another maneuver, for she slid down his body, then grasped his erection through his pants.

Colby looked at her in something he was certain resembled alarm.

Without taking her smiling gaze away from his, she unzipped his fly and put her hand in his pants.

Colby's heart raced, and his erection throbbed, rearing toward her seeking hand.

"Why are you doing this?" He was surprised at how hoarse his voice sounded.

"Lighten up, Still. Don't you ever have any fun?" She found the erection and grasped it.

Colby could feel her many rings, hard and smooth, against the skin of his shaft.

She worked it out of his boxer shorts and the fly of his pants, which was not difficult, for it was straining to free itself. She continued to smile at him as it stood rampant.

"Ah," she said and giggled. "Talk about standing for a principle." She winked at him, then lowered her head and took him in her mouth.

Thirteen

I do not allow myself to think about Kathleen. Does that
constitute thinking about Kathleen? The days pass slowly, as
they often do in the early stages of an organizing campaign.
I find myself at the end of one particularly long day when
Ken relieves me at the front desk. I wander back into the
work area, trying to look like I have some security business
back there, secretly hoping I might somehow run into
Kathleen, even though I know she is working across the
street.

The work area is in such disarray as to be nearly
unrecognizable. Cacophonous construction sounds come
from behind the blue tarp that hangs to the floor from
somewhere above the ceiling in the back half of the building. A portion of the ceiling back there has been removed.

A man walks past holding a small aluminum step ladder. He has a leather belt holding several hand tools, and he
wears safety glasses, a hard hat, and hearing protection. He
approaches a young man at a desk, taps him on the shoulder, and speaks to him. Although he has to shout to be
heard, I cannot understand his words from my position
twenty feet away.

The young man gets up from the desk and stands back.

The man in the hard hat pushes the computer monitor
and keyboard to one side, then opens his step ladder in

front of the desk. He takes one step up the ladder, then another on to the desk. He stands on the desk, pokes one of the ceiling tiles aside, and begins to grapple with something in the dark space above.

The young man, looking bewildered, wanders away. I go over to the water cooler, a spot from which I see Bryce at his desk, working under the watchful eyes of the serial killers whose pictures line the walls of his cubicle. I fill a paper cup with water and sip at it. I am near the blue tarp here, and the puling power saw behind it is the most irritating sound I have ever heard in my life.

Suddenly the saw shouts "Krang!" as it strikes some resistant element in the wood. The sound sends a shock up my spine, and I see the other employees in the vicinity stiffen in the same instant.

The power saw stops and a deathly silence descends on the room. I notice the paper cup in my hand is crushed and the front of my shirt is wet.

I see an employee stand up. There is an overturned mug on his desk, and a pile of papers is soaked with coffee. The employee walks over to Bryce's workstation. He leaves something near Bryce's elbow, and I recognize it as a membership card. Bryce looks up, nods to the other employee, and slides the card into his desk drawer. In a moment, a second employee has followed the first.

It occurs to me that nothing helps an organizing drive like the presence of carpenters and a blue tarp.

I throw the crushed cup in the wastebasket and wander off toward Kathleen's desk. Whatever caused the bone-chilling sound has apparently damaged the power saw, because it does not start up again.

Kathleen's desk is covered with plaster dust, and it is

apparent no one has sat at it all day. It looks as lonely as I feel.

"Hi, Gregg."

I turn, and Kathleen is standing behind me. She looks fetching, if a little severe, in a beige business suit. Her shoes have low heels, but they are leather and not like the brightly colored high-top sneakers she usually wears. Even her earrings are businesslike – little gold studs.

"Hi." I speak almost as quietly as if she were a deer ready to take flight at the slightest sign I might seek to injure her.

"What a mess this place is." She steps over to the desk, pulls her desk drawer open, bends over, and rummages in it.

"Yeah," I say. "What a mess." Is there no profundity I can muster?

She begins pulling papers out of the drawer and putting them in a leather portfolio. When she seems to have all the papers she is looking for, she puts the portfolio aside and rummages some more. Then she straightens up from the desk drawer with a stick of lip balm in her hand. She uncaps it and begins applying the stuff to her lips. Then she turns to leave.

"Wait," I say.

She turns back toward me, still circling her mouth with the balm stick. How can she put on lip balm when I am standing here? How can she act as if she is not in the presence of a man who wants her more than he wants anything? How can she fail to acknowledge that she has touched something deep inside me? She caps the lip balm and holds it out toward me. "Want some?"

I take the lip balm. I uncap it and apply it to my lips.

But it has nothing of her in it, and I am disappointed. I recap it and hand it back to her. "Kathleen, may I see you this evening?"

"I have plans for this evening," she says.

She turns to leave, and of course I understand very well what her plans are. She has detected in Stillman Colby an opportunity, and Kathleen is not one to miss an opportunity.

Fourteen

Colby stopped at the hotel coffee shop on his way to the office. Kathleen was still upstairs in the shower. She had made them both late this morning, refusing to let him shower alone, insisting on sex under the spray.

A vaguely remembered problem tugged at the edge of Colby's awareness, but when he tried to focus on it, it slipped out of his grasp. His heart quickened when he remembered sex in the shower: the water pelting his back, Kathleen, her wet hair plastered against her head, smiling and squinting against the spray. A laughing joy had swept over him as she approached her orgasm and shouted.

"Oh, Still. That's massive!"

Her declaration made him come until he nearly fainted. It didn't matter that she probably didn't mean by it what anyone else would, that *massive* was an all-purpose word in her unique vocabulary. Any man would relish the experience of that remark.

He asked the waitress for two coffees to go. Kathleen liked her coffee with cream. Cheeseburgers, fries, cream. It wasn't a very healthy diet, but she seemed an extemely healthy person. He wondered how she managed it.

But Colby himself wasn't used to these high-fat foods. This was nothing like the way he ate at home with Frannie.

The thought of Frannie focused his mind on the

vaguely remembered problem. He had not spoken with his
wife in several days. In twenty-four years, this was the longest he had gone without talking to her. Twenty-four years.
A sluice gate opened in the back of his mind and flooded
him with memory. He was twenty-seven years old, and he
was sitting in a small, brightly lit restaurant of spartan
decoration. Across the blond table from him sat an attractive young woman in business clothes and short hair. They
shared a large salad with chunks of avocado and a bitter-
tasting dressing.

"What kind of name is Stillman Colby?" Frannie put a
forkful of salad in her mouth.

"It means gentle man from a dark village." Colby
shrugged. "I looked it up when I was a teenager."

Frannie chewed for a moment, then swallowed. "I'm
not surprised," she said. "What a name for a kid to live
with."

Colby laughed. She was the most direct person he'd
met in the weeks he'd been at Tetraplan Insurance, and he
found her refreshing. And her insistence on eating in this
vegetarian restaurant was a new experience for Colby, too.

"But it suits you," she said.

"Which part?" he said. "The gentleness or the dark
village?"

"Both," she said. "You're considered quite a mystery
around the company, you know." Her eyes sparkled, and
Colby could feel a bond take shape between them that was
almost palpable.

"Don't people know I'm here to stop a union?"

"Until now," she said, "we didn't know how you were
going to do it."

"And now you know?" he said.

"Sure," she said. "You're going to charm them over dinner."

They chewed in silence for a while. The interminable chewing struck Colby as the principal disadvantage of vegetarianism. Who had time for all this mastication?

"What do your friends call you?" she said at last.

"They usually call me Cole," he said.

"I think I'll call you Still."

Colby laughed at the ridiculousness of the name.

"Why did you ask me to dinner, Still?" she said.

"Interviewing you was enjoyable, and I thought we might like each other's company."

"How do you know I'm not a member of the union?" she said.

"It wouldn't matter if you were," he said.

"Oh no?"

"It's just business, Frannie."

"Have you no principles?"

Colby smiled to keep the remark friendly, but he was serious. "That's not funny," he said.

"You started it," said Frannie, a little defensively.

"I'm sorry," said Colby. "I shouldn't have said it that way. It's just that my principles are important to me."

"What kind of principles allow you to be so cavalier about what you're doing?"

"I'm principled about service to my client," said Colby.

Frannie smiled and shook her head, as if to say she thought it was a principle he would eventually outgrow.

But he hadn't.

Frannie and the salad receded back into his mind as he approached the door to his office suite. Juggling the cups of coffee, he opened the door with some difficulty and found

Kathleen at her desk. Her hair was still wet and hung in ringlets around her head. She was talking on the phone.

"Four o'clock? Yes, I'll tell him." She made a note on a pad next to the telephone, put the handset back in its cradle, and looked up at him.

"Oooh, coffee."

"And a bagel." Colby set her cup and the wrapped-up bagel on her desk.

"My benefactor." She uncapped the coffee and immediately began sipping at it.

"What's at four o'clock?" he said.

"Harv's office called." She put down the coffee, unwrapped and attacked the bagel. "He wants to see you." With typical Kathleen intensity, she descended into the coffee and bagel, and although her body remained at the desk, her mind was completely preoccupied with the enjoyment of eating and sipping.

Colby had a feeling similar to the one he got when he watched Buster rolling in some unidentifiable offal. It was impossible to comprehend the intensity of the feelings being experienced, but it was easy to appreciate the pleasure.

He went into his office and sat at the desk, sipping at his coffee.

Kathleen walked past the doorway with a manila folder in her hand.

Colby could not keep himself from smiling.

She looked over and saw that he was smiling and paused in the doorway. She touched a dab of cream cheese on her lip and licked it off her fingertip.

Colby felt himself being aroused. He also felt a little ridiculous as they smiled at each other without speaking.

"Let me tell you a story," he said.

"Is this another story about an unfledged MBA?" she said.

It took Colby a moment to figure out the word *unfledged*. He wondered where Kathleen had gone to school. "As a matter of fact, it is," he said.

She smiled broadly, as if learning more about Colby's past was what she had been hoping for.

"The unfledged MBA was on assignment to an insurance company," said Colby.

"The same company?"

"A different one," he said. "The company's management said they had seen signs of organizing among the clerical and support staff, and the MBA was brought in to learn the extent of the union's strength. Most of the clerical and support staff were women, so the young man spent all day interviewing women. In retrospect, it would have made more sense for the company to assign a woman to the work, but managers don't always see these things."

"Tell me about it," said Kathleen.

"The young man found the organizer, but before he could do anything about it, he was involved in a relationship with her."

"This is beginning to sound roseate," said Kathleen.

Colby ignored the strange word. "The young man realized he had been compromised," he said, "so he asked his employer to reassign him."

"Did they?"

"Yes. They put him into a different insurance company."

"What happened to the organizer he had a relationship with?"

"He married her," said Colby.

* * *

Looking back on it, Colby understood that when you are intimate with a woman, it's not a good idea to tell her – even indirectly, by means of a story – that you have been married for more than two decades. And yet, the revelation seemed to have no effect on Kathleen whatever. She was as genial, as flirtatious, as unreserved in her speech and her feelings as she had been before the story. A remarkable young woman.

It was the last hour of the working day, and the FOW reception area was relatively quiet when Colby walked in. Seeing Gregg Harsh at the front desk made Colby remember Frannie again.

Colby felt uncomfortable around Harsh. Ordinarily, he would have taken this as a message from his intuition that Harsh was involved with the union. But he knew he had personal issues with the young man, and he could not tell where his personal feelings ended and his intuition began.

Harsh smiled at him. "How is it going, Mr. Colby?"

"Making progress," said Colby, even though he really wasn't.

When Colby opened the door to the work area, the air was filled with the music of reconstructive work. Colby was comforted by the sounds of power tools and carpenters shouting to each other. If Lathrop was building walls and partitions, nothing but good could come of it. It was the first step toward order and responsibility in this place.

The desks in the work area were much more closely spaced than before, but many of them were already empty near the end of the work day. As he threaded his way among them, he came across one employee who had plugged her uncovered ear with a fingertip while she shouted into the mouthpiece of a telephone receiver. And he found another sitting at his desk staring at a blank screen. He could not understand it. They should be ebullient with anticipation.

Harvey Lathrop's desk was not where Colby had last seen it. There was no desk there, just a blue tarp hanging to the floor from a point somewhere beyond the tiled ceiling. In this area, the floor was covered with power cords, plugged in to every available outlet but snaking under the tarp to power the construction equipment. In the narrow gap between tarp and floor, Colby could see piles of lumber and sheet rock. The workmen were apparently all behind the tarp, and Colby could find no way to reach them, short of crawling on his hands and knees under it. Fortunately, before he resorted to that, an employee, picking his way among the power cords, directed him to the second floor.

As the elevator carried him up, the construction noise did not recede. The doors opened, and Colby stepped into a brightly lit corridor with a blue tarp hanging vertically at the end. The sound of power tools was as loud here as downstairs.

To his left was another corridor with a cartoon on the wall. A smiling bear carrying a parasol. A couple feet along, there were more cartoons: a giraffe, a clown, and an elephant. And a few feet beyond that, there were even more: friendly lions, zebras, camels, monkeys.

The images increased in frequency as he progressed down the corridor. They finally became a mural, so that the entire wall was covered: three rings, horses with feathered headdresses, a ringmaster, ladies in sequins, trapeze artists, an audience, more clowns. In the center of the mural was a door. There was a makeshift sign on the door: "Dr. Harvey

Lathrop, CEO." Colby thought he called himself President. He wondered what this new title might mean.

Colby opened the door. A young man sat behind a desk, wearing a necktie and talking on the telephone. There was a computer monitor and keyboard on the stand beside him. It had a calendar on its screen. The door closed behind Colby, and the sounds of the power tools receded into the distance.

"He needs you for about forty minutes," the young man said into the telephone.

He turned to the computer, tapped something into the keyboard, then hung up. Turning to Colby, he looked a question at him.

"Is Harv here?" said Colby.

"Do you have an appointment?"

There were a couple of doors in the back wall, and before Colby could answer, one of them opened. Lathrop appeared in the doorway. He looked different. The lenses in his glasses were gray this time, and his hair was cut short and neat. His suit looked less liked he'd slept in it, although he had a growth of beard. He was carrying a piece of paper. He walked over and laid it on the young man's desk.

"I'll need this before the end of the day," he said.

The young man nodded, took the paper, and put it in a copy holder next to his keyboard.

"Cole," said Lathrop, "I'm glad you could make it. A friend of yours is here." He turned and headed back toward the door he'd come out of.

Colby followed his client.

"This is just temporary." Lathrop walked into the office. "Until they finish the renovations."

Colby was about to congratulate him on his campaign to bring some order to the place, when he came upon

Dennis seated in a chair in front of Lathrop's desk. Dennis stood up.

"Hello, Cole."

The two shook hands warmly.

"Dr. Lathrop tells me you've got a lot of activity going on across the street," said Dennis.

Colby glanced at Lathrop, whose eyes were unfriendly behind the gray lenses. Colby's intuition told him there had been a sea change. The man wasn't "Harv" anymore. He was "Dr. Lathrop."

"It's tough going, Dennis," said Colby. He didn't elaborate, because he didn't want to describe in front of Lathrop what a mire of structureless, irresponsible confusion this organization was.

"It's tough everywhere." Dennis sat again. "We got a call from a man who runs a franchise truck rental office in Forestdale. It seems the organizer has visited him, too."

Colby took a seat.

"We're getting calls from all over the place," said Dennis. "A dentist's office in Stroudsburg, an architect in Hackettstown, an ISP in Milford. This guy is everywhere. It's a dangerous situation. We're counting on you, Cole."

"I need back-up."

Dennis shook his head. "Not a chance. We're maxed out with other clients. This organizer knew what he was doing. He timed his campaign of terror to coincide with the busiest season we've had in years."

The three of them sat in silence for a moment while Dennis's information sank in.

"Could we talk about this site?" said Lathrop.

Dennis nodded toward Colby.

"I think we're in good shape, Dr. Lathrop," said Colby.

The other two waited for him to continue.

"I've located influential employees in every department, and I have taken steps to ensure their loyalty with subornation fees."

"Do you still think payments are the way to do this?" said Lathrop.

The "issues" again. Lathrop was obviously struggling with the need to embrace the ways of his enemy. Colby's heart went out to his old adversary.

"Dr. Lathrop," he said, "you have to avoid taking any of this personally. This IBOL organizer is not trying to take your union away from you. He's staging a direct attack on your members."

Lathrop nodded.

Sometimes you simply have to step in and give the client what he needs to win an argument with himself. "The members of the FOW rely on you to protect their interests. They want their union to provide the services it is supposed to provide, not get mired in contract negotiations, formal work procedures, and excessive pay scales."

Lathrop seemed to understand, for although he retained the scowl on his face, he nodded thoughtfully.

Colby judged it a good time to press his advantage. "It may take a little bit of getting used to, sir, but you need to consider acting like a corporation."

Lathrop's scowl intensified.

Colby knew there was a wise man he could quote on this subject. "A corporation," he said, "operates from a charter so generalized that it can change the nature and objectives of its business without amending it. As long as it operates within the law, it can change from manufacturing to service and back again without rechartering. It can change its location at will, and it is answerable only to its owners."

Lathrop obviously recognized his own ideas if not his words.

"That's the kind of freedom you must assume for yourself in waging this fight," said Colby.

Lathrop nodded, and Colby knew he was getting through.

"How many times have you gone up against employers who would stop at nothing to keep you out?" said Colby.

"More times than I can count," said Lathrop.

"I would bet that you learned something from each and every one of them," said Colby. "I've done this before. Our firm has stopped dozens of unions, but we need your support."

"What happens if this one can't be stopped?" said Lathrop.

The three of them looked at each other, and Colby felt the silent recognition that such an outcome was unthinkable.

"We haven't lost yet, Dr. Lathrop," said Dennis. "And we won't, not with Cole on the job."

Lathrop looked at Colby, and his eyes behind the gray lenses were not confident.

Colby smiled.

Lathrop did not smile back. "When will you know which way it's going to go?" he said.

"We know it's going to go our way, sir," said Dennis.

"Another two to three days," said Colby.

"About as long as the renovations are supposed to take," said Lathrop.

"We have to be going, Dr. Lathrop." Dennis stood up.

Colby stood as well. He could think of nothing more to say.

"Everything is under control, sir," said Dennis. "We'll be in touch soon with a progress report."

"Please do," said Lathrop.

Colby followed Dennis out of Lathrop's office. They walked past the young man's desk, which was now empty, and went into the deserted corridor where they could talk. The workmen had apparently left for the day, for the building was quiet.

"Dennis," said Colby, "this job is shaping up to be much bigger than we thought."

"You're up against one shrewd bastard," said Dennis.

Colby wondered if he meant Lathrop or the organizer. "Why are you here? Are you checking up on me?"

"Just following orders. Lathrop's," said Dennis. "And I have some information for you."

Colby waited while Dennis took out a piece of paper from his inside jacket pocket.

"It's not much, given what you're up against right now," said Dennis. "But we pinpointed the origin of the threatening faxes. They came from a rogue website that anonymizes fax transmissions. Our forensic specialists analyzed the data traffic on the server. The faxes originated from the FOW's own network."

"You're right," said Colby. "It's not much."

"Well," said Dennis, "at least it tells us the organizer is here on site. That narrows it down, and if you can undertake some unobtrusive surveillance, you might be able to identify him."

"Surveillance," said Colby, and he realized he knew someone on site who read everyone's mail.

* * *

Colby returned to the hotel feeling guilty. Should he have told Dennis that he had been having sex with one of the union executives? He told himself that he was capable of making the judgment call because he was close to the situation. He had never been closer to a situation in his career, at least since he'd met Frannie. Had he crossed the line?

He shouldn't bother himself with such questions. The next step was to get the information out of Kathleen about who the organizer might be.

He needed information from her, but he would have to be careful not to scare her.

When he entered his room, the bedroom door was open, and he could hear someone splashing in the bathtub. He went through the bedroom to the bathroom doorway and looked in.

Kathleen was lying in a tub full of water, wearing nothing but the small tattoo on her hip and a pair of gold hoop earrings.

Colby's pulse quickened.

"It's wash day, Still." Her smile raised her cheeks up under her eyes and wrinkled her nose. "And you're the laundry."

"Come on out of there, Kathleen," he said. "I have to talk with you." He turned and began removing his jacket as he walked back out toward the bed.

He heard her rise from the water and step out on to the tile floor. He stood in front of the bed and folded his jacket in half at the collar and tail. As he began to drape the folded jacket across the foot of the bed, he heard Kathleen's rapid footsteps on the carpet behind him. Before he could turn around, he felt her wet, naked body thump against his upper back and fasten itself there like a backpack. He was off balance, and he fell on to the bed with her lips fastened

to the upper ridge of his ear and one of her earrings pok-
ing into his neck.

They lay on the bed, and he could feel the globes of her
wet breasts soaking through the back of his shirt.

She took her mouth off his ear and whispered in it.

"I'm out. Do you still want to talk?"

He struggled to get up from the bed, but Kathleen was
agile, and he only succeeded in turning around so that his
head was between her breasts. His shirt was completely
soaked, and he could no longer remember what he wanted
to talk with her about, for his face had found the smooth
underside of her left breast. He licked the shallow crease
where the globe of her breast joined her ribcage. A tiny bit
of water that had been held there trickled on to his tongue.

Kathleen said nothing, but reached down and began
loosening his necktie.

He managed to kick off his shoes as he moved his face
up her side and into her armpit.

She giggled and finished pulling the necktie loose, then
snapped it from his collar and tossed it to the floor. She
unbuttoned his collar button and pulled him from her armpit so she could kiss his chest.

After that, he slipped his suspenders over his arms.
Then they both set to work peeling the soaked shirt from
his torso. His pants were easily unfastened and slipped off,
as they were still somewhat dry, and he found himself naked
except for his wristwatch and socks, lying on a wet bedspread.

Kathleen turned, straddled his chest, and leaned down
toward his feet to take his left sock off.

As she leaned down, the wet, dark fleece between her
legs rose and neared Colby's face. He pressed his mouth to
it and began to stroke her lips with his tongue.

She moaned as she got the sock off his left foot. She didn't bother with the right one, and instead seized his erection and licked it with her wet tongue.

For Colby, no world existed beyond the wet bedspread, her swelling genitals, and the feel of her velvety mouth.

She rubbed herself rapidly against his face, and her body shook.

She lost some of her concentration, and Colby felt the hard edge of her teeth against his shaft. It only ratcheted his excitement another notch. He kept the caresses of his tongue in rhythm, but he extended its explorations deeper.

Then she stopped shaking and rolled off him. On her back, she spread her legs and drew her knees up toward her breasts. "Get in," she said.

Colby rose to his knees before her, pulled her buttocks up on his thighs, then entered her.

She gasped.

She put the soles of her feet against his chest, and he watched her nipples shrink and harden as he began to thrust rapidly into her. "Like that?" he said.

"Yes yes yes," she said. "Oh, God, Still."

She began to shake and moan, the sign of one of her magnificent orgasms.

Colby did not try to count them, but she had several before his own finally started. When it came, it was volcanic.

When the eruption had spent itself, he fell over on the bed beside her.

They lay without speaking for a time. The combination of fatigue and relaxation lay heavily on Colby, but he knew he still had work to do. "There's something I have to talk with you about."

She propped herself on an elbow and began tracing

patterns on his chest with her index finger. "Should we get something to eat?"

Kathleen's appetite appeared to have no limits.

"I need to talk to you about some things first," said Colby. "The IBOL organizer has been sending faxes from the FOW network. That means he's on site. Your mail database may offer some clues about him."

"Melissa Willard called while you were at your meeting today," she said.

"What did she want?"

"The leasing company messed up her timesheets, and they are trying to blame it on her."

"Why is she calling us?"

"She thought since you're her friend, you might advise her. She's afraid Irene Gettings is going to fire her."

"She thinks I'm her friend?" said Colby.

"Aren't you?"

"What makes her think that?"

"You saved her job for her, Still. Of course you're her friend."

Colby was amazed at her naïveté. "I'm not her friend. I was just doing my job. It's nice that it helped her out, but I hope that doesn't make her welfare my obligation."

Kathleen lost her smile. "Does that mean you're not going to help her?"

"What could I possibly do to help her?" said Colby.

Kathleen looked thoughtful, but she didn't answer.

Colby was just as happy to have an end to the discussion.

"Can you run some reports on the mail database first thing in the morning?" he said. "If we can find the organizer, we can crush this thing."

But Kathleen still looked thoughtful. "What are we doing here?"

Again the issues. It seemed to Colby that he was spending an inordinate amount of time helping these people through their internal conflicts. He spoke softly but with feeling. "The members of the FOW rely on you to protect their interests," he said. "They want their union to provide the services it is supposed to provide, not get mired in contract negotiations, formal work procedures, and excessive pay scales."

Kathleen looked at him strangely. "You told me that once before."

"Did I?"

"And now that I think of it, I've heard you say the same thing to other people."

"Everybody around here seems to need the same counseling," said Colby.

"Is that what you think?" said Kathleen. "That I need counseling?"

Colby didn't say anything. He sensed this was going badly.

"I thought you were helping resolve some questions that were blocking me, but you weren't helping me. You were telemarketing me. Everything you told me was from a script."

Colby realized it might be time to write a new hand-holding speech. "Does that make it less true?"

"I'm not talking about truth," she said. "I'm talking about sincerity."

Colby didn't understand the distinction, but he realized the conversation was getting into dangerous territory.

"You don't even know the difference, do you?"

"Calm down, Kathleen."

Kathleen's voice was quiet, but it had a menacing quality. "You bastard. I thought you were just fucking me in bed. You've been fucking me tropologically, too."

"Tropologically?"

"You're as bad as Harvey Lathrop," she said. "You use people. You're a user."

Colby realized she was confirming his suspicion. She'd been intimate with Harvey Lathrop. There was too much to counsel her on. "Let's talk about this in the morning."

Kathleen stood up from the bed and walked out of the room.

Colby heard soft, rustling sounds from the other room, and he judged she was getting dressed. He should try to stop her. He might not be able to get her to run the reports tomorrow if she remained upset. He got out of bed and walked to the doorway.

Kathleen had already donned a pair of panties and a blouse.

"Kathleen," he said.

She looked at him.

The fucking was your idea. The words formed in Colby's mind, but his intuition told him not to say them. Winning an argument with her was not the way to get her to run the report on the database.

"I'm sure you have a prepared speech for this," she said. "Don't bother." She pulled on her slacks and stepped into her shoes. "It's not your fault. It's mine, for forgetting who my friends are."

And she left.

Colby watched the door close behind her. He doubted she would show up for work in the morning. Maybe he'd be able to find someone else to run the reports. He went to the closet and took out the terry cloth robe the hotel had provided. He put it on and sat down in the chair next to the telephone. He wished he could talk with Frannie right now. He sighed heavily, then dialed his own number. It rang four times, then the machine answered.

His answering message played. When it finished, he called to her. "Frannie? Are you there?"

There was no answer, and finally the machine beeped to indicate he'd reached the end of his allotted time.

Fifteen

I estimate Frannie to be about twenty years older than I. She has the slightly desiccated look of the active, aging vegetarian, but she is not unattractive. I wonder what Stillman Colby could want that he cannot find at home. It's not difficult to imagine being at home with this woman. She is self-possessed and confident, and there is a look in her eye that bespeaks hidden depths of passion.

She and I sit in my hotel room and chat while we are waiting for the organizing committee to arrive.

"Does he know you're on site yet?" she says.

"I don't know." I realize I have to confess to her that I have lost my conduit to Colby's operation. "I don't know what's happening with him. I had a contact in his office, but I lost that." I try to sound as businesslike as possible.

"It sounds like it was a close contact," she says.

Apparently I have not kept the feeling out of my voice.

"I got involved," I say.

"Nothing wrong with that," she says. "As long as you didn't lie to her. Women hate being lied to."

"I wish I'd talked with you a week ago," I say.

She looks at me curiously.

"Before I lied to her."

She laughs. "Maybe she'll forgive you. Women do hate

being lied to, but they're also used to it. Just tell her the truth. That's your only chance to fix it."

The organizing committee are buoyant when they arrive for the meeting. To meet their combined quota of thirty cards, they have brought us forty-three. With childish delight, they spill a pile of cards from a bag on to the table, and invite Frannie and me to inspect them. I defer to Frannie. She quickly looks over half a dozen of the cards and smiles at me.

"You two have done exceptional work," she says.

"It's Lathrop," says Lauren, her head bobbing excitedly. On my advice, she has taken to wearing her hair in green spikes. I have convinced her that people will feel more at ease with her if she dresses and grooms herself more conventionally.

"He's the best unionizer we could hope for," says Bryce.

"We must have gotten twenty new members," says Lauren, "just for his shutting down the daycare center. He's using it for his new office." She takes as much pleasure in it as if it were a great strategic move on her part rather than a blunder on his.

"These cards are perfect," says Frannie. "Completely filled out and witnessed. You two are good at this."

Bryce and Lauren look as proud as medalists, and it occurs to me they are involved in something that they have not known until now – a mission larger than themselves.

Seeing their eagerness, I find myself hoping for an early election. I feel that if we can file an RC petition with 95 percent of the workforce, we will win the election with almost no follow-up effort. We are more than halfway there. With a successful election, I can leave here and set about the task of getting Kathleen out of my mind.

Frannie clears the membership cards from the table, and the three of us tuck into our sandwiches while Frannie eats a tired-looking pear she retrieves from her bag. Our meal is like a dinner among old friends: talk, laughter, inside jokes.

I get great laughs from Lauren and Bryce when I ask them about the bonuses they have secured from Stillman Colby. They have taken my advice and accepted the money even while they continue to seek IBOL memberships. It is a great joke for them, and we all enjoy it tremendously.

We are the team that won the series, we are the crew that won the race, and we are so filled with barely restrained hilarity that I keep expecting us to break into a food fight.

"Is this the best organizing fight you've seen or what, Gregg?" Bryce smiles, and he drinks deeply from his orange soda.

I know it's not over until IBOL signs a contract with Lathrop, but this mood will prove useful to me. I need to find just the right combination of hope and realism to sustain their confidence while preparing them for obstacles. The sense of triumph and joy they feel now could carry us through the rest of the fight.

Frannie sees this, too, and tells one of her instructive stories.

"In the 1930s, unions were making so much trouble for General Motors it cost the company a million dollars a year to monitor its workers," she says. "They didn't have good employee monitoring in those days. They had to hire watchers and pay off some of the workers to report on union activity."

The two of them nod. It sounds familiar to them.

"But a million dollars a year wasn't enough. The union came in and signed up a handful of workers, then went to management and demanded to be recognized. Management laughed them off. But they didn't know who among all the workers had signed up, so they just had to sit tight and wait for some of them to slip up and show themselves.

"But these union guys were smart, and none of them slipped up. In fact, the union got their members into critical positions along the assembly line at a GM factory in Flint, Michigan. They called a strike, and when a few men stopped working on the line, it stopped the whole line."

"Didn't the company just replace them?" says Bryce.

"They couldn't. The union men wouldn't leave. They sat down on the job."

"Is that what they call a sit-down strike?" says Lauren.

"Exactly."

"Couldn't the company get the police to drag them out of the factory?" she says.

"The strikers took over the factory. When the police went in after them, the strikers drove them back under a hail of car parts. Then the strikers' families came and surrounded the factory, and passed food into the men through the windows.

"The strike went on for forty-four days. GM wasn't producing any cars during the busiest season, and the company lost so much money that management finally had to settle with the strikers. They signed a document recognizing the union. We finally had a full partnership in the industrial revolution – right about the time it was over."

"And it was downhill from there?" says Lauren.

"It took about fifty years for the corporates to put us down again," she says. "In 1981, thirteen thousand air traffic controllers walked off their jobs in protest over unsafe procedures, equipment, and conditions. The arms merchants, who were in control of the government at that time, told the President to lock out the controllers and hire new ones. The federal government decertified the air traffic controllers' union."

Frannie's story has an interesting effect on the young people. This is all new to them. They have no concept of history. The study of history is unfashionable these days. The expressions "that's history" and "you're history" mean "useless." I wonder if the corporates are somehow behind this. It certainly serves their purposes. They want us to have no memories, no context. They do not want to risk our having any knowledge against which to compare the information they supply.

Frannie takes the membership cards back into the bedroom, while I see Lauren and Bryce to the door. We agree to meet again in two days. I step into the corridor to say good-bye, and as the elevator door closes behind them, Kathleen rounds the corner. She is wearing a business suit, but a tail of blouse hangs over her waistband, as if she has dressed in a hurry, and her wet hair is disarrayed. She has not seen Bryce and Lauren, but she has seen me.

"Hi, Gregg," she says.

I am at something of a loss. It takes me a moment to realize that she doesn't understand the situation.

"Hi," I say.

"I didn't know you were staying here," she says.

"My place is being fumigated," I say. "The landlord put me up here."

"Heck of a landlord." She pushes past me into the room. "Nice room."

She seems to be familiar with the layout and goes directly to the table, where our stacked plates testify to a light dinner. "I guess you don't want to order a couple of cheeseburgers, do you?"

At that moment, Frannie walks out of the bedroom.

Kathleen manages to look at her as if she were an intruder, even though that is patently not the case.

Frannie, in her turn, looks at Kathleen with curiosity. "Are you with the hotel?"

"I was going to ask you the same thing," says Kathleen.

"Frannie," I say, "this is Kathleen. She works with me at the FOW."

"Did you bring a membership card?" says Frannie.

This is going badly.

I shake my head vigorously. "She's on assignment to our management consultant."

"Membership card?" says Kathleen. For the first time since I've known her, she appears to be nonplussed.

I see recognition in Frannie's eyes as she understands that this attractive young woman with the uncombed hair and untucked blouse is working for her husband. I expect the expansion of recognition to narrow to a squint of jealousy. But Frannie is a strong woman with a nimble mind, and if she has any feelings of jealousy, she does not voice them, even in her body language.

"Membership card?" says Kathleen again. But her bewilderment at Frannie's question is only momentary.

I can see comprehension light her eyes when she turns to me.

"You're the one, aren't you?"

I have spent the last couple years hiding from management and forming secret liaisons with employees, and at this moment I feel as uncomfortable as I can ever remember feeling. Tactical and operational problems are easy to deal with, but this appears to be an emotional one. If I say the wrong thing, someone is going to have their feelings hurt, and I realize with a start that it could be me.

"You work for Stillman Colby?" says Frannie to Kathleen.

"Up until a few minutes ago," says Kathleen. The state of her clothing and the edge in her voice provide her explanation.

I don't know what to do, and silence envelops us like the stillness at the eye of a hurricane. Then an inspiration emerges from somewhere deep inside me.

"How about those cheeseburgers, Kathleen?" I say.

"I guess I'll be going," says Frannie. She turns to Kathleen. "I'm a vegetarian."

I hardly notice Frannie leaving. I study Kathleen while she works out the implications of what she has learned. The door clicks shut behind Frannie.

"Frannie and I go back a long way," I say.

"Yeah, and you've never had a date," she says sarcastically.

"Frannie?" I laugh. "She's my mentor."

Kathleen reddens. "People get involved with their mentors sometimes."

"I'm sure they do," I say.

We both know what I am talking about.

She looks away, and for a moment I feel as if I've won an argument. But I know that I'd rather win Kathleen than the argument.

My voice, when I speak again, is soft as a whisper. "Why have you been avoiding me, Kathleen?"

She does not look at me.

"I need to know," I say more loudly.

She finally looks at me again, begins to speak, then stops herself. "Wait a minute. Why am I on the defensive?"

She begins to pace the room. It is the most serious I have ever seen her. "You're the IBOL organizer, aren't you?" she says. "And that woman is your mentor? Is she from IBOL?"

"Frannie's not with IBOL," I say, which is true. But I don't want to tell Kathleen that I am the entire staff of IBOL. I am its founder, its chief executive officer, its external organizer, its vice president of operations. "I met Frannie at the school where she works as a teacher. I was driving a school bus at the time." I don't mention that I successfully organized the school bus drivers into an IBOL local.

She sits on the sofa, and I am relieved to have her pacing stop. "You're not even Hmong, are you?"

I can think of no new lies, and furthermore I don't want to. Seeing her sitting there, I realize I want nothing so much as I want her. I open my mouth, but there is nothing to say.

I shake my head, then sit on the sofa at the opposite end from her. "I couldn't tell you who I am, but I wanted to be friends with you, so I made up a new identity."

She looks away, and we sit in silence for a moment.

"I'm third-generation Korean," I say. "I was raised in Ohio. My father, who is a banker, speaks a little Korean, but with an American accent."

She looks at me sidelong. "The real you this time?"

I nod, not wanting to risk her growing receptivity by speaking.

Some of her former friendly expression returns, and she actually seems gratified that I have gone to so much trouble to be her friend. "You didn't need to lie to me," she says.

"I hoped you'd like me," I say.

"Makes a lot of sense, Gregg," she says sarcastically. "You want a woman to like you, so you lie to her."

"It made sense at the time," I say. "If you knew who I was, you'd have to turn me in. Your job would depend on it."

She does not turn away again, so I slide closer to her end of the sofa. I take her hand. "I didn't want to put you in that position."

The black pupils of her eyes enlarge and crowd the golden brown irises to their edges. "You care about people, don't you?" Her voice is soft.

"That's why I do the work I do," I say. "You do, too. It's why you became a union activist in the first place."

I am not ready for her kiss, which hits me as unexpectedly as a blow to the face. She searches for my tongue with hers. She begins unbuttoning my shirt. The touch of her fingers on my bare chest gives me an erection. She pulls my shirt off.

She strips herself quickly. She has a blue-and-red tattoo on her lower abdomen. A teddy bear, about the size of a commemorative postage stamp.

She leans over me, kisses me again, and without understanding how, I find myself lying on the sofa with her on top of me.

"You've never had a date?" she says.

I think about Frannie's advice to start telling her the truth, but I can also tell she is fascinated by the idea of my virginity, and I don't want to spoil it for her. "I have, but it never got to sex."

Kathleen gets up and leads me to the bedroom, where she undertakes to teach me about sex.

"Touch me with your hands, baby," she says.

I have never been addressed as "baby" before. My heartbeat quickens inexplicably, and my erection enlarges.

"Softly," she says. "Like butterfly wings."

I explore the contours of her body with the pads of my fingertips, feeling not her skin, but the warmth of the air along its surface. My hands glide slowly over the smoothness of her ear, the artery pumping beneath the surface of her neck, the lattice of her ribs, the shrinking aureoles around her hardening nipples.

She sighs and leans over to kiss my ear. "Keep going."

It needs all my self-control to stop myself from pressing my hands to her sleek flesh, but I continue to let the tips of my fingers hover within a hair's breadth. I trace the rise of her protruding hip bone, the barely perceptible down below her navel, her tattoo. I do not need to feign awe; I am nearly breathless with desire and excitement.

She makes a soft cooing sound, then whispers to me. "Use your mouth, baby."

Her skin is like satin against my lips and tastes like soap to my tongue. I kiss and lick the dish of her abdomen cradled within the hip bones, then move to the insides of her thighs. I work my way around to the tuft of dark, curly hair between her legs, tugging it lightly with my lips, feeling for the flesh beneath it with my tongue. I touch my lips to hers, then begin to kiss and lick the swelling flesh, mindful of my role as butterfly wings. She coos again and allows me to lick gently at her lips for some moments, running her hands all over the back of my head. Finally, she begins to pull my head upward.

I let her pull me toward her face, and she grasps me at the back of the neck with one hand and kisses my mouth with hers, sending her tongue first to rub against mine then to explore my teeth. Her free hand strokes the nipples on my chest, and I am surprised at the excitement this gives me.

We are still locked in our long kiss when she grasps my erection. I no longer know whether I am kissing her, for all my awareness has focused on her touch. I have no mind, no thoughts, no self.

I have hardly entered before she begins to shake and moan uncontrollably. I begin to thrust. Her face strains as if she were hoisting a heavy weight. Her mouth opens and closes, but nothing comes out. Tears roll down her face. I thrust faster while she clutches my buttocks, pulling me into her repeatedly. She finds her voice. "Oh, baby. Oh, baby."

It is the "Oh, baby" that pushes me beyond restraint. I cannot withhold my ejaculation, and it rumbles toward my genitals like a tsunami.

My entire being is expelled with the semen – an orgasm beyond any I have known before. For an instant, I am unaware of anything other than the surge of my soul into her.

When my body finally stops shuddering, I am afraid I might weep. I manage to suppress it, but I understand how truly lonely I have been until this moment.

Sixteen

It was shortly after three, but Colby couldn't sleep and he felt he might as well go down to the office and get some work done. He was glad Kathleen wasn't in his bed. She was on the verge of becoming difficult, and he did not need that right now.

He had to re-tie his necktie three times to get the dimple centered below the knot. When he was happy with the result, he slipped his Brooks Brothers jacket on, picked up his copy of *The Noncooperative Economy,* and went out into the hushed corridor to the elevator.

The elevator played a lilting, string version of an old song Colby recognized as "Whole Lotta Love." The elevator reached the lobby, and the doors opened. Colby stepped out of the elevator. He saw a woman who appeared to be in her fifties sitting on one of the lobby sofas. She had the healthy glow of an active vegetarian, and she looked familiar.

Colby realized with a start that the woman was Frannie. He had not recognized her at first because he was not looking for her, and because after being married to her for more than twenty years, he still tended to think of her as the girl he'd met when he was twenty-seven. She was no less attractive now than she had ever been, but she looked

different: her blond hair was streaked with gray and her
face bore the lines of an energetic life.

She was looking directly at him, as if she'd been waiting for him.

She didn't get up when he walked over to her, and he
felt a little awkward as he bent over to hug her.

"What are you doing here?" He sat down beside her.

There was no one else in the lobby, and the insipid
string music from the overhead speakers somehow increased
the quiet.

"I had to talk with you, Still," she said.

Had she missed him so much that she drove down here
in the middle of the night? Colby was secretly pleased. "I'll
be home soon," he said. "I'm almost done here."

"More than you know," she said. "I shouldn't be showing myself to you like this, but I saw your little playmate
this evening."

"Playmate?" Colby sensed deep trouble. He understood
she had not come because she missed him. His secret
pleasure turned into a sinking feeling in the pit of his
stomach.

"Kathleen," said Frannie. "Isn't that her name?"

"Kathleen?" Colby wondered how long he could stall
her by repeating what she said.

"Cut the crap, Still," said Frannie.

Not long at all, apparently. Colby marveled that as
skilled as he was in controlling conversations and directing
people's behavior, Frannie had a knack for making him feel
like a child.

"I don't know what you're talking about," said Colby.
"Kathleen is the name of the vice president of operations at
the union I'm working for. The president of the union
assigned her to work with me."

"Did he assign you to untuck her blouse and mess up her hair and send her fuming around the corridors of this hotel?"

"What are you talking about?"

"I saw the girl tonight," said Frannie. "She was in a state of dishabille. And she spoke of you in tones a woman reserves for a man who has taken advantage of her. Is that what you're doing these days? Inappropriate contact with a subordinate?"

"She's not my subordinate," said Colby sullenly.

Frannie didn't say anything. She just gazed at him with disgust, as if he'd given her a sufficient answer.

He searched the last few lines of conversation in his mind, trying to find what he'd said that gave him away. "It was her idea," he said.

"You're worse than unprofessional," she said. "You're ungracious."

"Why won't you tell me what you're you doing here, Frannie?" he said helplessly.

Frannie stood up. "You'll find out eventually, and you'll be sorry."

"Frannie, don't leave," he said.

Frannie turned and walked away.

Colby stared at her retreating back, trying to comprehend that he had somehow lost his wife.

Then Frannie stopped, turned around and walked back. "If you want to know how it all ends," she said, "I'm quite certain she's up there sleeping with Gregg right now. And eyeball is going to kick the crap out of you on this one."

Sleeping with Gregg. Eyeball was going to kick the crap out of him. Colby turned this over in his mind as she turned and walked away again. This time she got to the lobby door, and walked through it.

A roar sounded, and Colby looked over to see a man pushing a vacuum cleaner over the carpeting.

Eyeball? Sleeping with Gregg?

The explanation, when it came to him, was fully formed. Eyeball was IBOL. Gregg was Gregg Harsh, the Asian security guard. Frannie, a union activist of long experience, was advising Harsh. Harsh was the IBOL organizer on site.

Seventeen

I am exultant. That is the only way I can describe it. I have fifty-two signed membership cards from FOW employees, and I have Kathleen.

Last night was as wonderful as it was unexpected.

We must have been quite tiresome for the room service waiter when he finally came in with the cheeseburgers. We hurriedly donned terry cloth bathrobes from the closet before I opened the door to let him in. Then we tried to act like the tense ASSes he would expect to find in this level of the hotel. But as he went about his business – setting out the cheeseburgers, retrieving the bill from his leatherette folder, asking for my signature – Kathleen and I looked at each other several times and burst out laughing.

The waiter affected not to notice he was in the presence of people far more giddy than warranted by the current state of the world. When he finally left, we seized the food he had so carefully laid out, took it over to the bed, and began feeding each other. By the time we had finished eating, the terry cloth robes were stained with ketchup and hamburger grease. The bedspread had french fry pieces mashed into it.

"So how long have you been organizing us?" she said.

"I took this job to organize the FOW from the inside," I said. "It's the first time I've tried it this way."

"Have you organized other sites?"

"My biggest job before this was a company in Boston called Growth Services," I said. "Around here, I've just gotten a few other places started. I've been doing this for a couple years."

"What did you do before that?"

"I was a management consultant," I said.

"That's an unusual career change, isn't it, Gregg?"

"Management consultant, union organizer," I said. "The work's pretty much the same. It's only the ideological superstructure that's different."

"So you had a sort of religious conversion?"

"Did you?"

She was thoughtful for a long moment. "Somehow the ends and the means got mixed up for me."

"Most people will tell you they act out of principle at all times," I said. "But we really just try to get through our lives and manage the situations we find ourselves in."

"What made you decide to organize a union headquarters?"

"What made you decide to work against it?"

"Still explained to me that we work for the members of the FOW, and he made it sound like it was disloyal to support any other union."

"And you bought it?"

"You would, too," she said.

"I'm sure I would," I said. "Colby and I actually have a lot in common."

"No, you don't," she said. "He's insincere, and a worm."

"Colby tries to make it safe for people to act only for themselves. I try to make it safe for them to act for others."

"That sounds like you're saying I worked with him because I'm selfish," she said.

"That's Colby's genius," I said. "He bribed you with the opportunity to help people."

Her bright brown eyes shone as her gaze played over my face.

"You're susceptible to that," I said.

She didn't say anything, but kissed me deeply, a prelude to making love again.

We were up for hours after that, just talking.

"Why did you leave Colby?" I said.

"He's an ASS," she said. Then she seemed to realize that didn't explain anything. "They're very selfish, you know. I think money makes them that way. I think maybe when people get money, they immediately forget what it was like not to have it. It disconnects them from the rest of us."

"You mean, it's impossible for people to relate to each other when money is present?" I said. "That sounds pretty deep."

"Everybody has a deep theory about life," she said. "That's mine."

"It's not a very positive view of human nature," I said.

"It's the twenty-first century, Gregg. Ninety percent of us are poor and getting poorer. Who is positive about human nature?"

"I am."

"Oh, yeah," She said. "You stalk businesses. You're real positive."

"I'm in the business of possibilities," I said. "I think anyone, shown the possibilities, will work to make the world a better place."

"Tell that to Harvey Lathrop," she said.

"That's exactly what I'm trying to do," I said. "Why do you think I'm here at the FOW? I think even a good-natured nitwit like Harvey Lathrop can make a contribution."

She looked serious then. "You've got Harv all wrong. He's not a nitwit, and he's not good-natured."

I sensed she was speaking from experience.

"He taught me a lot about human nature," she said.

I did not interrogate her about it. I just hugged her.

We made love once more. I was too exhausted to apply myself. Kathleen rolled me on my back and mounted me.

As I walk carefully across the highway toward the FOW building, my groin feels like it has been secured with knots of nautical complexity, but I hope for a full recovery by this evening.

I enter the building and there are people gathered around my reception desk. They have seen me, and it is too late to get away. There is nothing I can do but approach and hope to bluff my way through. Stillman Colby is sitting on my desk, with one wingtip-shod foot flat on the carpeting and the other dangling at the end of a bended knee. It is a pose of studied casualness, intended, perhaps, to throw me off my guard. Two other suited men stand beside Colby. One younger one and one about Colby's age. Colby and the other suit chat idly under the apparently watchful eyes of two men in dark windbreakers and sunglasses with tear-shaped lenses. The men in windbreakers are armed. Pinkerton goons.

Colby smiles as I approach.

"It's over, Harsh."

"What are you talking about?"

"We know it's you." Colby pushes himself up from my desk to stand in front of me.

The two Pinkertons step closer, until there is one standing on either side of me. One of them pops the fastener on
his holster to free his sidearm. Colby makes a cutting
gesture to him with his hand.

"He's not going to give us any trouble, are you,
Harsh?"

I start to back away, but I feel a hand on each of my
arms, like steel restraints.

"It will go easier on you if you don't behave stupidly,"
says Colby.

I realize the goons are at the peak of alertness. Struggle
would be futile.

"Cuff him, Axel," says the older suit, who appears to
be in charge of the Pinkertons.

One of the goons pulls a pair of handcuffs from a
holder on his belt. He comes in close to fasten the cuffs on
me, and I see that the skin on his face is smooth and he has
barely any beard. He could not be more than twenty-four.

"Harsh," says Colby, "the FOW has terminated your
employment here."

"On what grounds?" I manage.

"The FOW needs no grounds," says Colby. "You're an
at-will employee."

"Everybody gets riffed sooner or later, huh, Still?"

My gibe is successful. The color rises in Colby's face,
and for a moment I believe he may strike me. But the suit
in charge sees it, too.

"You've got him now, Cole," he says. "He's just taunt-
ing you. Like he did with the faxes."

"And like he did when he took your girl," I say.

This time Colby starts toward me. But the suit grasps
his arm.

"Don't blow it."

I can see the effort in his face as he gains control of himself, but apparently the older suit is a calming influence on him, because he appears to relax slightly.

Colby and I stand there staring at each other without saying anything, while the suit watches Colby.

I need to get word to Kathleen.

"Let me make a call," I say.

"No calls." Colby smiles, enjoying my distress. He turns to the suit in charge. "He's all yours, Dennis."

Dennis signals the other suit, who starts toward the door. The two goons lead me after him. They take me to an enormous black sport utility vehicle with darkened windows. I recognize it as a late model Ford Excessive. One of the Pinkertons opens the middle door and guides me in. I am handcuffed, and he must hold my arm to balance me as I step up into the vehicle.

The young goon who handcuffed me, Axel, climbs in and sits on the seat beside me. The other one climbs into the driver's seat, and the suit gets in beside him.

I don't know where they are taking me. I fight to remain calm.

The suit looks at me over the seat. "We'll leave the cuffs on," he says. "It's not that far."

I wonder if I will be able to persuade them to make a stop along the way.

Axel sits stiffly beside me. He is sweating, and I realize he is nervous.

The suit turns back to face the windshield and tells the driver, "OK, let's go."

Axel's sunglasses, lubricated by perspiration on his face, have begun to slide down his nose. He carefully takes them off, as if he is not used to wearing them.

"Responsible position for somebody in his first job," I say.

Axel turns to look at me. He has the wide eyes of a novice. "How did you know it's my first job?"

"I know because I remember my first job," I say. "I know what it was like and how it felt, and I recognize it when I see it."

Eighteen

Colby's anger gave way to something like relief as he watched the Pinkertons lead Harsh away. It was done. The FOW and the nationwide tier of medium-sized businesses were safe.

"What now, Cole?" said Dennis.

"I'm going back to my office to start writing my report," said Colby. "It looks to me like the FOW is safe."

"Before I return, I'll get a meeting with Lathrop to give him the news," said Dennis. "Do you know who he wanted to call?"

Colby thought about Kathleen. Now that Frannie had left him, he wondered if there was a chance of rekindling his relationship with her. "I don't know," he said.

He found Kathleen in the office, packing up her things. She was wearing the pink overalls again.

"You're early," she said. "I thought I could get out before you got here."

"I've got some bad news for you," he said.

She did not speak, just waited for him to continue.

"Dennis just took Gregg Harsh into custody."

It was the first time he had ever seen shock on Kathleen's face. She knocked over her coffee mug, spilling the dregs of her coffee across the desk. "Where did he take him?"

"You weren't involved in his organizing campaign, were you, Kathleen?"

She looked down and saw the coffee spreading across her desk. She reached across the desk to a box of tissues, took a handful, and began sopping it up. "Organizing campaign?"

"You know what I'm talking about," said Colby. "Harsh was the organizer for IBOL."

Kathleen didn't answer. She started toward the door.

Colby grabbed her arm. "Wait a minute, Kathleen. You owe me an explanation. Were you spying on me for him?"

She yanked herself free. "Are you kidding?"

"You could lose your job, Kathleen."

"Take it." She started toward the door again. "I'm leaving."

"You can't run away." He made a grab for her, but she danced out of his reach.

Colby felt foolish, and he could not decide whether to make another grab for her or let her go and send Pinkertons to pick her up later.

"Save yourself the effort, Still. You can't catch me without help."

Colby decided to reason with her. "The man's no better than a criminal. He turned my wife against me."

"Something you're really good at," she said, "is fooling yourself."

"I never lied to you," said Colby, as if that contradicted her remark. Then he remembered telling her the story about his made-up brother. "Well, not about anything important, anyway."

Kathleen laughed and turned to leave.

"Don't believe his propaganda, Kathleen. He's the enemy of working people. If he has his way, he will take

away their freedom of choice and tie them up with restric-
tive work rules. He has nothing to offer but bureaucracy."

"Tell that to the fifty-two people who signed membership cards for him," she said over her shoulder.

Fifty-two membership cards? That was at least two-
thirds of the bargaining unit. It hit him like a blow to the
face. Two-thirds of the bargaining unit. The FOW was a
hair's breadth from becoming a union shop.

Colby went to his telephone and dialed Lathrop's office.

Lathrop himself answered, and he sounded like he was
having a good day. "Lathrop here. May I help you?"

"This is Stillman Colby, Dr. Lathrop."

"Cole," said Lathrop with genuine friendliness. "I'm
sitting here with Dennis. Congratulations. I never would
have suspected Gregg Harsh. He was such a nice young
man. Very conscientious."

"They are always the ones you don't suspect," said
Colby. "They can even be charming sometimes."

"I guess you called to say good-bye," said Lathrop.

Colby steeled himself to deliver the bad news. "I think
we may have some trouble on our hands, sir."

Lathrop said nothing.

One thousand one, one thousand two, one thousand
three, one thousand four. Colby could stand the silence no
longer. "Sir, Harsh had already organized two-thirds of the
FOW's employees. That's more than enough to force an RC
election. It's only a matter of time before someone steps into
Harsh's place and calls you to ask you to recognize IBOL."

"How could this happen?" said Lathrop. His voice
became momentarily distant, as if he were talking away
from the receiver. "How could this happen, Dennis?"

Colby ignored the question, since it spoke directly to
his own competence. "Dennis will bring in some Pinkertons

in case the workers get violent. I think we can contain it. But it's important that you not talk to the union rep when they call."

Lathrop said nothing for a moment. When he spoke again, he did not sound like a man on the verge of losing his organization. "Do what you have to do, Cole. I am scheduling an all-employee meeting. It's time to remind them what we mean to each other."

"I don't think that's a good idea, sir," said Colby.

"We've tried it your way, Cole." Lathrop spoke in measured, managerial tones. "It's time to get back to fundamentals."

* * *

Colby went to the all-employee meeting the next morning. The employees were all filing into the main work area. The blue tarp was gone, revealing that at the back quarter of the building, the second and third floors had been removed, so that the area now formed a three-story atrium. It was topped with skylights, so the area was quite bright, in spite of the three-story drapes of teal and gold that covered the back wall. In front of the curtains, at a height about the middle of the second floor, there was a catwalk with an aluminum railing.

The employees all drifted toward that end of the build- ing. The floor of the atrium was teal-colored slate, and the area was bounded by a teal-colored velvet rope slung along a dozen shiny brass posts, like a nightclub to which they might not all be admitted.

Colby did not like this situation. Lathrop's best chance of stopping the union was to emphasize the workforce-as- family angle. You don't promote a family atmosphere by remodeling the work area into an upscale hotel lobby. This man had unionized so many organizations in his day. Why did he not see that he was acting just like the less-enlightened managers he'd worked against?

Colby wondered how Frannie was. And he wondered where Kathleen had gone.

The employees stood and chatted, and Colby sensed unease. They had all heard about Harsh.

Colby didn't know where Dennis was, but he supposed he had assembled a squad of Pinkertons and was keeping them out of sight, waiting to be called. Colby wondered what was going to become of his own tenure. He wouldn't blame Dennis for throwing him to the wolves. He didn't feel he had managed this assignment very well.

A chime sounded from the direction of the atrium. Everyone stopped talking and turned to look.

Plaintive, synthesized music emerged from somewhere, and the curtains behind the catwalk slowly parted, revealing floor-to-ceiling windows. Blinding sunlight poured in as the music shifted mood. It turned on itself, swelled, and emerged as an anthem of some sort. Colby could feel the hairs on the back of his neck rising. A chill passed through him and he felt the way he'd felt the time he attended an Easter sunrise service in church.

In the intense sunlight, he could barely see a figure striding out to the middle of the catwalk.

Colby tried to shade his eyes. The figure in the sunlight was about the size and shape of Lathrop. The music and the sunlight washed over him, and Colby recognized in himself the signs of suspended judgment. Music, sunlight, crowds of people, vaulted ceiling ... these were the elements of awe. Colby suspected everyone felt the same tingling he felt.

Colby did not particularly like Lathrop, but he had to admire his handiwork. This could be the solution.

The Lathrop figure raised a hand, looking like an Aztec priest at a sacrificial ceremony. The music stopped, and hush blanketed the room. The silence was so profound that Colby clearly heard the figure snap its fingers. The windows behind the figure immediately turned copper color and dampened the light to a friendly russet.

The figure was indeed Lathrop, although he was nearly unrecognizable. His head was shaved, the lenses of his glasses were mirrored, and he wore an Italian-cut suit – over a tee shirt. He looked around with the expression of the good guy at a professional wrestling event.

Colby fought an overwhelming desire to lose himself in the ceremony. By an enormous effort, he took his eyes from Lathrop and looked at the people around him. They all stared upward at the figure on the catwalk, like witnesses to an apotheosis.

"Good morning, ladies and gentlemen," said Lathrop. "Thank you for coming. There are issues we need to face as a community, and I've called you here to help me with them."

He spoke in normal tones, and Colby realized he had equipped himself with a sound system of some sort, so he could speak relatively softly and still be heard throughout the entire first floor.

"I understand," said Lathrop, "that some of you have signed membership cards for a labor union called IBOL." He pronounced the letters individually.

Colby searched the faces of the people around him. Fifty-two of them may be IBOL members, but at this moment they were all children of the FOW family, staring up at the spectral figure on the catwalk.

"The members of the FOW rely on us to protect their interests," he said. "They want their union to provide the services it is supposed to provide, not get mired in contract negotiations, formal work procedures, and excessive pay scales.

"You are such splendid young people, but I know there are unfortunate gaps in your education. I founded the FOW in the depths of the 1980s, when the labor union movement was marginalized. Most of you won't remember this, but before the 1980s, labor unions were identified with progress. In the 1980s, however, the corporates learned to use sophisticated public relations programs to identify us as an obstacle to progress. They hired scholars and researchers to create distorted theories and explanations about us. They manufactured stories of corruption about us and planted them in the news media, which they own. They bought elections for our enemies, and then used the pulpit of the government to denounce us." Lathrop looked from one side of the crowd to the other, taking them all in, and then continued. "In the end, it's not difficult to control public opinion.

"Once they had turned the public against us, the corporates went after us. They provoked us with job insecurity, pay cuts, dangerous working conditions. When the unions responded with strikes, they broke the strikes. Their lackeys in government began to whittle away our legal protections. Work site after work site was decertified, until finally the federal government destroyed the air traffic controllers' union. It was a low point for organized labor.

"It was then I founded the Federated Office Workers with a new vision of office workers in control of their own destinies. We would stand up for ourselves and demand job security and safe working conditions. There were only a handful of us then. I can't tell you how hard it was to stand up against the intimidation and the harassment, day in and day out. I paid my dues, ladies and gentlemen. I've put my life into this organization, and now outsiders are trying to hijack everything I've worked for."

Lathrop paused, and the room was so quiet Colby could hear the whisper of the building's ventilation. Lathrop had apparently transcended his internal conflicts, and he had done so with a vengeance. Colby had never seen a corporate put on this kind of show. In the hush, a solitary voice spoke.

"We've worked for it, too."

Lathrop looked over the crowd. "Who said that?"

"And we just want to stand up for ourselves."

Colby looked over toward the direction of the voice, and one of his influentials, Bryce, stood there in baggy shorts and baseball hat.

"Thank you," said Lathrop. "Of course you want to stand up for yourselves. The question is, do you want to give up the community we have here?"

"We just want a fair working environment," said Bryce.

Lathrop stood quietly for a long time, appearing to digest this. Finally he began to speak again.

"It is only by getting back to fundamentals that we can get our union back on track." Lathrop paused for effect. "Today, we shall have a sacrifice in order to bind our community together."

Lathrop's tone was utterly reasonable as he looked directly at the young man who had spoken up. "This sacrifice will be Bryce Reznik from the production team. Bryce, clean out your desk."

A gasp went up from the crowd as the import of this gesture sank in.

"See how much better the rest of you feel?" said
Lathrop. "You've still got jobs."

Colby looked toward Bryce, but far from cleaning out
his desk, he seemed to be climbing up on it. And on the
desk next to his, Lauren, her hair done up in green spikes,
jumped up and brandished a handmade placard with a
drawing of a stylized eye on it.

"We don't have to take this," she shouted. She slowly
turned around so that everyone could see her sign.

"Get down from that desk," said Lathrop.

Lauren stopped and turned toward Lathrop. "You're
not just dealing with Bryce," she shouted. "Talk to the
eyeball!"

"Lauren," said Lathrop, "If you don't get off that desk,
I'm sending in security."

Without saying a word, Lauren dropped her sign and
slowly sat down on the desk.

Colby heard a door open, and he turned to see a pair
of security guards enter. As they started toward the employees sitting on the desks, however, other employees closed
ranks in front of them and attempted to block their way.
The guards, facing several dozen unarmed but clearly hostile
employees, hesitated. The two of them looked at each other,
then turned and retreated.

"Get up from there, you two," said Lathrop. "Get off
those desks."

As he spoke, a young man dressed in a tee shirt and
baggy shorts climbed on to the desk next to Lauren's and
arranged himself cross-legged on it. Another employee
followed suit, then another.

As each employee found a desk to sit on, Colby decided
he had a bad feeling about this.

Nineteen

The four of us are in a motel room, where we have come to assess our situation and determine our next steps.

"Do you need anything?" says Frannie.

"Can you find Axel a job?" I say.

"What can you do?" she asks Axel.

"I can handle a gun," he says eagerly, "and I know how to use handcuffs and restraints. But I don't want to do that anymore."

"He probably won't be able to get a good reference from the Pinkertons, anyway," says Kathleen.

Frannie looks at Axel. "Can you do anything else?"

Axel is thoughtful for a moment. "I've always wanted to be a teacher," I say.

"I can help you there," says Frannie. "Are you willing to work as a substitute while you study for your certification?"

"A substitute teacher?" says Axel. He speaks as if Frannie has the power to grant his dream.

Frannie looks at me. "Can you stake him a few weeks' expenses?"

"That's no problem," I say. I have already retrieved my emergency funds. Before we leave the area, Kathleen will clean out her bank accounts. We will be quite flush.

Frannie turns back to Axel. "You'll be coming with me, then. I know a suburban school district that could use a muscular substitute teacher. We'll get you into night school for your certification studies."

Axel and Kathleen go off into a corner of the room whiile Frannie and I chat a little longer. We avoid talking about Colby. She says she has decided to go on the road. "It's been a long time," she says. "But I think I'll remember how to do it. I'm looking forward to it."

"Do you want to come with us?"

"I don't think that's a good idea," she says. "You have Kathleen, and I would just slow you down."

I wish her luck, and we look over at Axel.

He and Kathleen are bent over an open cardboard box. Frannie and I go over to them. "What are you doing?"

Kathleen turns and wraps her arms around my neck. "We're packing up Axel's gun to send it back to Pinkerton. We can't stand its egregiosity."

"I'm going to feel a little funny without it." Axel takes the handcuffs from the holder on his belt and tosses them into the box after the gun.

"Where do we go now?" says Kathleen.

"We'll mail Axel's package in Forestdale, and you can get whatever you need from your apartment and bank accounts."

Axel grabs my hand impulsively and shakes it. "Thanks for everything, Gregg." He is grinning. "Just think. Me, a teacher. Nobody's ever going to tell me, 'Cuff him, Axel' again."

By the unspoken laws of the fugitive underground, Kathleen and I do not ask about the "suburban school district" where Frannie is taking Axel, and Frannie does not ask us anything about our destination.

Frannie turns to Axel. "We'll stop at a men's store and get you a new jacket, so you can throw away that windbreaker with the Pinkerton logo."

The two of them leave.

"What about us?" says Kathleen.

"I don't want to stay in Forestdale," I say. "I've been considering a real estate management firm in Wilmington and a website designer in Newark. I could take one, you could take the other. Do you want website designing or real estate?"

"Websites," she says.

"There's a truck stop I want to look in on before we leave this city behind."

I embrace her, by way of asking for sex. She is eager and responsive. It is clear to me that I have only a short time with her. Whether I tell her or she hears it from a news report or an old friend, she will eventually learn that Bryce and Lauren were the ringleaders of the "situation" at the FOW. And she will know that I used her to identify them when she was working for Colby. It will be an ugly scene, and she will leave. This drama between Colby and me will close with no one getting the girl.

Twenty

Lathrop took over Colby's office in the Select Suites hotel. The sit-down strikers did not seem particularly violent, but Dennis was afraid that if the CEO remained on site, he would become a hostage.

The three men met in the office, and it was Colby's first chance to talk with Dennis since he'd arrived with the Pinkerton strike force.

"Did you get anything out of Harsh?" said Colby.

"Harsh got away." Dennis looked embarrassed by his revelation.

"What happened?" asked Lathrop.

"They stopped for fuel about halfway to headquarters. He asked to use the rest room, and they let him. I thought they were better trained than that. The agent in charge sent the other agent with him. A kid named Axel."

"He overpowered the agent?"

"I don't think so," said Dennis. "When the others went in to look for them, they were both gone. My guess is, Harsh talked Axel into helping him escape. Then he promised to make Axel a big-time union official or something."

Colby couldn't criticize the Pinkertons. How could they know how persuasive Harsh could be? When they took him away, nobody had any idea how far things had gone at the FOW.

"I don't know how they got away from the rest stop, though," said Dennis. "Where did they get a car?"

"Did they see anyone else at the rest stop?"

"It was a rest stop, Cole. Of course there were other people there."

Colby realized Frannie must have been in the parking lot when they took Harsh away, and she followed the van in her car, ready to take him away if he tried to escape. He gave Dennis a description of her to add to the descriptions of Harsh and the Pinkerton.

"I want your people stationed around my building, and I want them there permanently," said Lathrop. He looked directly at Colby. "We have a situation here, and your firm is responsible for it."

The implication was not lost on either Dennis or Colby, but Colby thought it rather ungenerous of Lathrop to put it that way. He was, after all, the one who wanted to play sun god.

* * *

Colby went back to his hotel room. He was at a loss, and he thought maybe rest was a good idea. The room was annoyingly empty and lonely. *The Noncooperative Economy* was lying on the desk, but he couldn't bring himself to open it.

Instead, he lay on the bed, fully clothed, and took a fitful nap. His wife was gone. His lover was gone. His enemy was missing. He'd been removed from his assignment. He felt quite alone.

He had no idea how long he'd been lying on the bed when he heard the knock on the door. He got up hopefully and looked through the peep hole. Dennis was standing there.

Colby opened the door.

"I have bad news for you, Cole."

Dennis looked haggard.

Colby waited.

"You've been riffed."

Colby felt less shock than he might have expected. "What happens now?"

"The firm will cover your hotel bill until the thing across the street is settled. After that, I'll give you a lift home."

Less than a week ago, Colby had a generous salary, a sports sedan, responsibilities, a wife at home, and a girlfriend. How could a man lose so much so quickly?

"I'm sorry, Cole," said Dennis. "It was Lathrop. He said I had to let you go. He's the client."

Colby was sorry, too, but somehow it was comfortable to be Lathrop's adversary again.

"Lathrop's cut off power to the building," said Dennis.

"What are your agents doing?" said Colby.

"They are camping on the grounds to form a blockade. Lathrop doesn't want anybody going in to resupply them."

* * *

Once Dennis left, Colby felt like he was under house arrest. He couldn't concentrate enough to read or watch television. He couldn't do anything but pace. He challenged himself to find the longest possible route around the room, walking along the walls and circling the furniture.

He could see the FOW building from his window, and occasionally he stopped pacing and watched. But he couldn't tell much from the activity he saw: men with weapons watching the building, climbing in and out of Excessives, talking into radio headphones.

Eventually, he was tired enough to lie down. He slept fitfully and awoke in darkness. He got out of bed and went to the window. The FOW building was dark except for the searchlights trained on its windows. There was very little activity around it.

Colby heard a knock on the door.

It was Dennis.

"They want to negotiate," he said.

"Did you come to get my advice?" said Colby.

"More than that," said Dennis. "They asked for you. Lathrop says he'll give you one more try."

Colby wasn't entirely surprised. The influential employees he'd worked most closely with appeared to be the strike's ringleaders. He'd had them on a special payroll. They probably felt that if they'd taken advantage of him once, they could do it again.

"What terms is Lathrop offering?" said Colby.

"If they come out now, he won't gas them."

Gas. "Just let me get my coat," said Colby.

As he walked across the highway with Dennis to the FOW building, Colby tried to nurse his resentment of Lathrop for restricting his negotiating position. He hoped that by concentrating on the frustration, he could keep fear out of his mind.

The low building looked sinister. Dark inside, it was crisscrossed with the high-intensity beams of the Pinkertons' floodlights. From the outside, there was no sign of life.

Dennis took Colby through the rank of Pinkertons and toward the door. "They said to step inside the door and wait for instructions."

Colby nodded. With his heart pounding, he approached the door, pulled it open, and stepped inside. He pulled his topcoat tighter. It was no warmer in here than outside. His breath emerged in steamy puffs, which were brightened by the floodlight illumination from outside. He looked around.

The lobby was a study in contrasts. Parts of it were plunged into utter shadow, but the floodlights at the windows made other parts of it as bright as a television studio. Light glinted from the brass FOW logo on the wall behind the reception desk.

A voice spoke from the floor behind the desk.

"Approach the reception desk, Mr. Colby."

Colby walked up to the desk. "You can call me Cole."

"Fine, Cole. Do you see that shadow toward your left behind the desk?"

Colby nodded, then realized that whomever he was talking to probably couldn't see him. "Yes."

"Step into the shadow."

Colby did as he was told. His eyes weren't used to the darkness, and he could see nothing within the shadow. Hands touched him, then patted him down.

"He's not armed," said a man right next to him. "This way, Cole."

A shadowy figure led him through darkness to the door into the work area. As they stepped inside, Colby saw the strangest scene he had ever seen in his life.

The atrium at the end of the building was dark, for the strikers had apparently closed the three-story curtains. In the gloom of the work area, half the desks had shadowy figures sitting on them. As they neared the desk sitters, Colby was able to see that some were in shirtsleeves and others wore coats.

"It's cold in here," said Colby. "Why are those people in shirtsleeves?"

"We have pooled our clothing," said his escort. "We wear it in shifts."

The place did not look like living quarters. There was no litter, and it was clear that the strikers took some pride in its neatness. As his eyes adjusted to the darkness, Colby could see that there was nobody in the atrium. They all stayed in the work area, as if in some strange way they were remaining on the job.

Many people sitting on desks were eating from small packages. Colby's fear subsided as he saw how peaceful the place was.

He and his escort passed a desk that was piled with small packages like the ones people were eating from, and the packages were being distributed to a short line of workers by two people.

"We pooled our pocket money and bought everything in the vending machines," said Colby's escort, who then added, "before they cut off the power."

Colby had to admire the ingenuity with which they had stretched their endurance, but he knew they couldn't last more than a week, even if Lathrop made no effort to eject them.

His escort took him to the desk where he'd seen Lauren hold up her placard during Lathrop's all-employee meeting, which now seemed a lifetime ago. Lauren and Bryce sat on the desk, talking quietly.

"Welcome, Cole," said Lauren. "You remember Bryce?'

"Why did you ask for me?" said Colby. "To rub it in or what?"

"Gregg said if we ever got into this situation, we should

try to involve you," said Lauren. "He said we could trust you."

"I don't understand," said Colby.

"What he actually said was, we could trust your vanity," said Bryce.

Lauren looked at him with irritation, and it occurred to Colby that the two of them must feel they were under a great deal of pressure. "Bryce is too blunt," she said. "Gregg thought you would work harder to settle it than anyone else might."

This was supposed to be a negotiation, and Colby didn't want to show any emotion, but he felt like shaking his head ruefully. Based on his performance to date, if he was the best the prevention community had to offer, the world was destined to be heavily unionized.

"You could settle this thing, Cole," said Lauren. "Talk them into recognizing the union, and we'll all go back to work."

"Even if I wanted to," said Colby, "I don't have the latitude. They are going to give you two choices."

"What are they?" said Bryce.

"You can leave now, or you can get gassed," said Colby.

"You can't believe it's a good idea to gas us, Cole," said Lauren. "And they certainly won't, as long as you're here."

If his situation had not been so serious, Colby would have laughed. Lathrop would be pleased to gas him along with everyone else. He suddenly understood the vindictive bastard's plan. No wonder he'd allowed Colby to negotiate. He realized there was nothing he could do but wait for the gassing.

Lauren handed him something.

"What's this?" said Colby.

It was a card, about five inches by eight inches. He took it and held it sidelong to catch the ambient light. He recognized the IBOL logo: a stylized human eye over the name International Brotherhood of Labor. Below that was an identifying headline: MEMBERSHIP APPLICATION.

"I am a prevention and decertification specialist with the country's foremost labor relations consulting firm, and you want me to sign a union membership card," said Colby. "I have to ask you, are we living on the same planet?"

"Same planet," said Lauren. "A pretty crazy one, isn't it?"

Colby realized he was deeply touched. He was their sworn enemy, and they were asking him to join them. That's what life is about, when you reduce it to its essentials. Without trying to, he thought of Buster back at Kimi Pond, and how Colby had trained him by acting as if they were a two-dog pack. The Federated Office Workers, Republican Party, American Civil Liberties Union, Boy Scouts, everybody wants you to join their dog pack. Lauren was right. It was a crazy planet.

It was strange to have this realization in this situation. Sitting in this cold, dark building, he felt closer to these two people than he felt to Lathrop. He felt closer to them than he felt to Dennis. But he had no desire to join their dog pack.

"I'll take it under advisement." Colby put the card in his coat pocket.

"Think about it," said Bryce. "There's time."

"No there isn't," said Colby. "Lathrop is going to gas you, and he is perfectly happy to have me with you when he does it."

The two strike leaders were silent for a moment. Finally Bryce spoke.

"He wouldn't do that. He won't have a union without us."

"He cares less about that than he cares about winning," said Colby. "You've managed to turn him back into a corporate. The way he sees it, he can't win unless you lose."

They heard a great crack from overhead, followed by the strangely musical sound of tempered glass breaking. There was a hail of glass in the atrium, and Colby understood that the skylights had been shattered. Canisters, about the size of soup cans, began to land on the floor. They issued wispy tendrils, which rapidly turned into plumes and gouts of unpleasant-looking vapor.

In moments, the building was filled with a stinging fog.

Colby heard people coughing and shouting. His eyes and throat burned and he began to cough uncontrollably. He tried to make his way through the fog and his own tears to the door. Other people had the same idea. Colby couldn't see, but he followed the crowd noise until he thought he detected a draft of fresh air. He stumbled in that direction until he was aware of passing through a doorway, coughing and crying. He knew he had emerged into the reception area. He could hear the sounds of the workers' coughing mingling with barked commands of Pinkertons. He struggled to open his eyes.

Through a blur of tears, he saw that the reception area was crowded with people. A man in dark clothes approached him. He was elongated like an El Greco painting, which Colby attributed to the distortion made by his tears. But the man had an enormous, misshapen head. Then Colby realized he was wearing a gas mask. He stepped up to Colby and reached out to him with a device of some sort.

Every muscle in Colby's body seemed to contract at once. There was a buzzing in his ears, and he felt like he'd fallen into a tub of thumbtacks. He was grateful when his mind shut down.

Twenty-one

Colby didn't have much to pack for the drive back to Kimi Pond: a handful of suits he had worn in rotation during the assignment, his underwear, his razor and toothbrush. He left the copy of *The Noncooperative Economy* on the desk in his room. He was glad to say good-bye to it and the hotel. He looked forward to resuming his simple life in the woods.

As he approached the Excessive sitting in front of the hotel entrance, the door opened for him. He leaned in and threw his bag over the seat into the back. Dennis sat at the wheel.

Colby said nothing as he climbed in.

"Are you feeling better?" said Dennis.

Colby settled himself against the leather upholstery.

"It's a fairly long drive," said Dennis. "You might as well talk a little."

Colby didn't want to talk to Dennis, but there was something he wanted to get off his chest. "I know we've always said that tear gas and stun guns are humane because they are nonlethal," he said. "But having been on the receiving end, I don't think they're very humane at all."

"I'm sorry you went through that, Cole, but you'll forget about it soon."

"No I won't." Colby pulled down the shoulder harness and buckled himself in.

Dennis turned the Excessive's ignition key, and the engine roared to life. He put the car in gear and they headed toward the Throughway.

They had exhausted their conversational inventory, and Colby could feel a great distance open up between them, too far to even shout across.

They were cruising smoothly on the highway when the telephone in the center console deedled.

Dennis pressed something on the steering wheel. "Yes," said Dennis.

A familiar-sounding but unplaceable female voice emerged from a speaker in front of the rearview mirror. "Is Stillman Colby there?"

Dennis glanced over at Colby.

Colby pointed at the receiver in the console, miming a request to speak with the caller privately.

Dennis nodded.

Colby picked up the receiver and held it to his ear. "This is Stillman Colby."

The woman's voice was friendly.

"Mr. Colby, this is Melissa Willard."

Colby didn't recognize the name.

"I'm the manager of Jolly Jim's Refresh & Refuel," she said.

"Of course," said Colby. He barely knew her, but she was a friendly voice to a warrior returning home in defeat. He felt genuinely pleased to be speaking with her. "How have you been?"

"I've been very well," she said. "Today is my last day at Jolly Jim's."

"That's too bad," said Colby.

"No, it's not. I haven't been happy here. The employees are losing some of their benefits under the leasing arrangement, and I don't like being a part of that."

Colby couldn't really blame her. "Where will you go?" he said.

"I got a job managing the local Flashburger," she said. "They were unionized recently, and the owner fired the manager."

"That's usually the way," said Colby.

"I think it's a good situation," said Melissa. "The owner decided to bargain with the union. I think I'm going to like working with people who have some control over their working lives."

Colby had never thought about it that way before.

"But that's not what I called about," she said. "You asked me to call if I saw any strangers talking to Alan. I promised to do that, so I'm calling you now."

"What did you see?" said Colby.

"There's a red sport utility that has been out in our parking lot all night. This morning, when Alan's shift ended, I saw him go over to it. He's there now, talking with a Asian-looking man and a young woman in colored overalls."

Colby looked at his watch. If he told Dennis, they could be at Jolly Jim's in half an hour.

Harsh and Kathleen. They had wrecked this assignment. In a way, they had destroyed everything he had worked for. Now he was returning to Kimi Pond, alone. He had no job, no car, no money. He would pass the rest of his days trying to tease some meaning from old books, walking along the edge of the pond, training his dog.

He thought about Lathrop. He thought about the young people in that dark building. They told him they could always trust his vanity. And with a clarity borne of his suffering, he suddenly understood they were right.

"Mr. Colby?" said Melissa. "Are you still there?"

"Yes," said Colby.

"Do you need any more information from me about these people?" said Melissa.

"No," said Colby. "No, I don't. Those people are friends of mine. Nothing to worry about. Good luck in your new job."

She thanked him and said good-bye.

He pressed the key to break the connection, then replaced the receiver in the console.

"Anything important?" said Dennis.

"No," said Colby. He felt in his coat pocket and found the IBOL membership card. He pulled it from his pocket and looked at it. The strikers must have thought he would be an asset to their dog pack.

"What's that?" said Dennis.

"Nothing," said Colby. The scenery hurtled past outside, but the Excessive ran so smoothly it was the only evidence that they were moving.

"Dennis," he said, "do you have a litter bag in this thing?"

Floyd Kemske is the author of five novels, including the three other Corporate Nightmares, *Lifetime Employment* (1992), *The Virtual Boss* (1993), and *Human Resources* (1995), as well as the historical novel *The Third Lion: A Novel About Talleyrand* (1997), which presents a wry look at the essence of the man who helped make and break both the French Revolution and Napoleon. When he is not writing fiction, Kemske is the editorial director of Kaplancollege.com, the professional education and career services website. He lives in Pepperell, Massachusetts with his wife and dogs.

This book was set in the Sabon face and printed by Quebecor World in Fairfield, Pennsylvania. The jacket was printed by Strine Printing in York, Pennsylvania. The photo on the front cover is the work of Ron Chapple. The author photo is the work of John Paul Kowal.